D1627137

DOG TROUBLE!

DOG TROUBLE!

Galia Oz

Translated by Gilah Kahn-Hoffman

CROWN BOOKS
FOR YOUNG READERS
NEW YORK

All rights reserved. Published in the United States by Crown Books for Young Readers, an imprint of Random House Children's Books, a division of Penguin Random House LLC, New York. Originally published in Hebrew in hardcover by Keter, Israel, as *Shakshuka Disappears* (2007), *Shakshuka Strikes Again* (2008), and *Shakshuka and the Awfully Dreadful Cat* (2011).

Crown and the colophon are registered trademarks of Penguin Random House LLC.

Visit us on the Web! randomhousekids.com

Educators and librarians, for a variety of teaching tools,
visit us at RHTeachersLibrarians.com

Library of Congress Cataloging-in-Publication Data is available upon request.
ISBN 978-0-399-55020-1 (trade) — ISBN 978-0-399-55022-5 (ebook)

Printed in the United States of America
10 9 8 7 6 5 4 3 2 1
First American Edition

Random House Children's Books supports
the First Amendment and celebrates the right to read.

To Alon and Yael,
for bringing the smile
into this book

CONTENTS

SHAKSHUKA DISAPPEARS

CHAPTER 1

My puppy, Shakshuka, disappeared. It happened when my dad was away on a business trip and my mom was in one of her worst moods ever because Max and Monty had both just had their vaccinations and they both had reactions and they didn't sleep all night. Max and Monty—I called them the Munchkins for short— were babies and twins and also my brothers, and everyone knew that if there were two babies in the house, no one was going to pay any attention to a dog, even if she was only a baby herself.

At night, I lay awake in bed and I was cold, and I remembered that once on TV I saw pictures of a hungry dog that was really skinny whose family went on a vacation and left him tied to a tree. And they said that the SPCA couldn't take care of all the dogs that were abandoned by their families. And I thought about Shakshuka, who was gone and might be tied to a tree at that very minute, hungry and missing me.

●　●　●

The next morning in class, Brody told me there was no way that Shakshuka had been stolen. "No way, Julie!" he said. "Why would anyone bother? You could get five dogs like her, with spots and stripes, for less than ten dollars." Or maybe he said you could get ten dogs like her for less than five dollars. Brody said things like that sometimes, but most of the time he was okay. When Max and Monty were born, he said that was it, no one at home would ever pay attention to me again, and when I cut my hair short, he said it was ugly.

I turned my back on Brody and pretended to listen to Adam. He sat at the desk next to mine and spent his whole life telling these crazy stories.

Adam said, "My father won f-f-fifty thousand, do you get it? In the lottery. He's g-going to buy me an i-P-P . . ."

People didn't always listen to Adam because he stuttered, and they didn't always have the patience to wait until he got the word out. This time Brody tried to help him finish his sentence.

"An iPod?"

"N-not an i-P-Pod, you idiot. An i-P-Pad."

Brody called Adam "Ad-d-d-dam" because of his stutter, and because he liked to be annoying. But he was still my friend, and that was just how it was, and anyway, there were lots of kids worse than he was.

I cried about Shakshuka during morning recess and Danny laughed at me because that was Danny, that was just the way *he* was, and Duke also laughed, obviously, because Duke was Danny's number two. But at the time I didn't know that they had anything to do with Shakshuka's disappearance and kept telling myself that maybe they were just being mean, as usual.

That Danny, everyone was afraid of him. And they'd have been nuts not to be. It was bad enough that he was the kind of kid who would smear your seat with glue and laugh at you when you sat down; that he and his friends would come up and offer you what looked like the tastiest muffin you'd ever seen, and when you opened your mouth to take a bite you discovered it was really a sponge. But none of that was important. The problem was, he remembered everything that anyone had ever done to him, and he made sure to get back at them. The day before Shakshuka disappeared, Mrs.

Brown asked us what a potter did, and Danny jumped up and said that a potter was a person who put plants in pots, but Mrs. Brown said that was not what a potter did. And then I raised my hand and said that a potter was a person who worked with clay and made pottery.

Danny, who sat right behind me, leaned forward and smacked my head, and I said, "Ow." It wasn't too bad, but the teacher saw him and she wrote a note he had to take home to his parents. That shouldn't have been so bad either, but later, when school got out, he grabbed me in the yard and kicked me in the leg. I went flying and crashed into the seesaw, where I banged my other leg as well.

Danny said, "If you hadn't said 'Ow' before in class, the teacher wouldn't have given me a note. Now because of you I'm suspended. That was my third note."

Our school had this system that every time a kid hit another kid, he got a note he had to take home to his parents, and if it happened three times his parents had to come to school and the kid got sent home. My mother said it was mainly a punishment for the parents, who had to miss a day of work and come to school.

I could have told on him for kicking me in the yard as well. My bag flew off my shoulder and landed right in the middle of a puddle, and Mom was really angry at me when I got home because we had to take out all the books and leave them out to dry and we had to wash the bag. I really could have told on him, but there wouldn't have been any point. It would just have meant another note for him, another kick for me.

Thanks but no thanks.

● ● ●

In the evening, when the Munchkins went to sleep, Mom took one look at me and burst out laughing and said she wished that you could buy a doll that looked just like me, with scratches on her right knee, black dirt under her fingernails, and a mosquito bite on her cheek.

"It's not a bite, it's a bruise," I told her. "And anyway, who would buy a doll like that?"

"I would," said Mom. "But what happened to you? Take a look at your legs—how on earth . . ."

"Ow! Don't touch."

"You look as if you were in a fight with a tiger."

That was so close to the truth that I blurted out the whole story about what happened with Danny. And I was really sorry I did that because that was the reason Shakshuka disappeared. Mom spoke to Mrs. Brown and she must have told her I was black-and-blue after Danny pushed me because the next day at school Mrs. Brown took me aside and told me that I had to let her know whenever something like that happened because otherwise Danny would just keep on hitting me, and other kids too, and we had to put a stop to it. Mrs. Brown meant well, but I knew that when it came to Danny, I was on my own.

Later, at the end of the day, Danny caught me again, this time when I was right by the gate. Maybe someone saw me talking to the teacher and told him. Suddenly I was lying on the ground with my face in the dirt. I must have shouted because Danny told me to keep quiet.

Then he said, "Tell me what you told Mrs. Brown!"

"Let me get up!" I yelled.

"First tell me what you told her."

"Let me get up!" My neck was all twisted, but somehow I managed to turn to the side and I saw two first graders walking out of the building toward the gate.

Danny must have seen them too because he let me go, and when I stood up he looked at me and started laughing, probably because of the dirt on my face, and I decided I'd had enough of this jerk. I saw red, no matter where I looked I saw red, and without thinking about what grown-ups always taught us—that we shouldn't hit back because whoever hit back would be punished just like the one who started it—I threw a plant at him.

At the entrance to our school there was this huge plant. The nature teacher once told us that it grew so big because it always got water from this pipe that dripped down into it, and also because it was in a protected corner.

It was a shame about the plant, it really was. And it didn't even hit him. It crashed to the ground halfway between us. Then Mrs. Brown came. And without even thinking I told her that Danny knocked me down and then threw the plant at me.

"But it didn't hit me," I said, and I looked Danny straight in the eye to see what he'd say.

Danny said I was a liar, but Mrs. Brown took one look at my dirty clothes and she believed me. And because of me he got into serious trouble. They didn't only make his parents come to school and suspend him for a day—after the incident with the plant they also told him he'd have to start seeing this really horrible counselor every Wednesday. The kids who knew him said his office stunk of cigarettes and he was a real bore.

That was why Danny found a way to get back at me. He said, "Just you wait." That was exactly what he said: "Just you wait." And I did wait because I knew him. But Shakshuka didn't wait and she couldn't have known how to wait for what ended up happening to her.

CHAPTER 2

The day after Shakshuka disappeared and we'd already searched for her all over the neighborhood, we sat at Brody's house and Effie came over. Brody lived on the floor above me, and Effie, who was my cousin, lived opposite us. She came over sometimes to play with us. Effie could run really fast, faster than any of the boys, and in the afternoons she went to all kinds of activities, like Learning How to Survive a Disaster. But she never opened her mouth in class and she was never a part of things. I liked Effie, but I didn't always have time to pay attention to her.

I told Effie and Brody it must have been Danny

because Shakshuka disappeared just a few hours after he promised to get even. Brody said it wasn't that easy to steal a dog. You had to put it somewhere and it made noise, and then your parents asked where you got it. "But what if he just left her somewhere?" I asked Brody, and I couldn't help thinking again about the dog I had seen on television, tied to a tree.

Effie didn't say anything. She just stared at the screen saver on the computer. Brody said that Shakshuka was probably out there somewhere, making friends and eating food from garbage cans. She loved everyone, that Shakshuka.

I'd only had her for a couple of weeks, ever since she showed up in the yard of our building when we were playing there, and Mom said, "Julie, I don't have the energy to take care of anything else, even if it's a plant." But Shakshuka was nothing like a plant. She never stopped moving and wagging her tail and wriggling and she licked Max inside his mouth and he actually really liked that and he shouted "Da!" and Monty was a little scared at first, but then he started crawling around following her and pulling her tail. Mom said that the next time that dog put her tongue in a kid's mouth she was going to teach her a lesson she'd never forget. But Shakshuka wasn't impressed at all— she immediately turned to Max and licked him and we all laughed, even Mom. When Dad came home he thought she was great and he wanted to take her to the vet to get her shots, but then he went off on another business trip. In the two weeks I'd had her I didn't even manage to memorize all her spots and stripes, so I was trying to remember them now.

Apart from Effie, Brody, and me, only Brody's grandmother was at home, which was usually fine because she was always in the living room watching TV or sitting on the balcony and staring at the yard. But then Effie and I got bored sitting in Brody's room and watching him score points in his computer game, so we went into the living room.

Brody came out and asked his grandmother to change the channel, and she looked at him with her huge eyes, which always looked even bigger behind her glasses, and said, "But he's talking. You can't interrupt him while he's talking."

"He's just an announcer, Gran. He's reading the news."

"He's talking to us right now, and you can't interrupt him," said Brody's grandmother. "It would hurt his feelings."

Brody's grandmother was sure the announcers on television could hear what we said and she worried about hurting their feelings. Sometimes Brody and his sister, Nina, got into this crazy mood and they started annoying the announcers on TV.

"Not *her* again! I'm tired of seeing her face every time we turn on the TV. Can't we watch something else?" Nina jumped up and covered the television screen with a cushion, and Brody's grandmother shouted, "That's enough! Sha! Quiet! Such rudeness!"

Sometimes it ended with Brody's grandmother cursing in Russian, and then Brody burst out laughing and started a pillow fight with Nina, and that was when Brody's grandmother took the opportunity to apologize to the announcers. And sometimes she got really angry and said, "Because of you, she went away."

"She didn't go away because of us, Gran. She went because the lady who does the weather forecast told her to go away," said Nina.

Brody's grandmother thought all the neighbors were eavesdropping on her through the pipes. And yesterday evening she stood on the balcony and shouted that there were thieves outside. She was sure she had loads of enemies. She really was a poor thing and it wasn't right that Brody and his sister made fun of her, even though Brody said it was also a way to give her some attention.

"Besides, we're not laughing *at* her; we're laughing *with* her," said Brody.

I never believed it when people said that.

And you couldn't laugh with Brody's grandmother anyway because she never laughed. I guess she didn't have much of a sense of humor. I wasn't sure Effie had a sense of humor either. Once, when the three of us were playing in Brody's living room, Effie stared at Brody's grandmother for a long time and then said out loud, "What's wrong with her? Is she talking to herself?"

But Brody's grandmother wasn't talking to herself. She was talking to the wall. Actually, she was talking to the picture hanging on the wall. And that was a lot less strange than talking to yourself.

And just before we left Brody's house, Effie said, "You know, he was here yesterday evening."

"Who?"

"Danny," she said calmly. "Danny was here with Duke."

Effie, who Brody always called Space-Effie, was half asleep most of the time, even when she was awake. I'd never seen anything like it. She told us that yesterday she came back around seven from her class on Creative Baking Outdoors and she saw Danny and Duke coming out of the yard. They walked down the street and she went into her house, and that was it.

Effie couldn't understand why Brody and I got so worked up. She couldn't see why it was so important.

No, she hadn't seen Shakshuka. She only saw Danny and Duke running. "Hold on," said Brody. "A second ago you said you saw them walking."

"Well, they were running," said Effie, "running like mad."

Effie didn't have much of a sense of humor. They said animals didn't have a sense of humor either, but my Shakshuka had one. Of all the shoes in the house, she decided to chew up the slippers that had clown faces on them—well, mostly the right one, where the clown's face looked a bit scarier. I loved those slippers, but I loved Shakshuka even more, especially after she chewed up the one with the scarier face.

Mom actually got angry with Shakshuka. She didn't care about the clown faces, but it was obvious that if a dog started chewing kids' slippers, it wouldn't be long before it got to the grown-ups' shoes, and Mom had great shoes, it was just that she never got to wear them since Max and Monty were born. Mom said that the next time Shakshuka touched a shoe, she'd chop ten inches off her tail.

When I got back from Brody's house, I yelled at Mom, "It's your fault she's gone! Why did you let her out in the yard?"

And Mom said, "Why didn't you take her for a walk, Julie? If you had taken her for a walk like you promised, I wouldn't have had to let her out on her own. She was howling by the door!"

I knew she was right. I should have taken Shakshuka out myself with the leash; then she wouldn't have been wandering around alone by the entrance to the building at about seven o'clock at night, and nothing would have happened. But still I kept shouting, "You're not even looking for her! You said you'd put an ad in the paper. You said you'd drive around in the car and ask people."

Mom said, "Maybe she belonged to someone else. Maybe she had owners and she went back to them. She's not ours yet. We still haven't given her her shots."

And then I shouted, "Why didn't you get her her shots?"

And Mom said, "Give me a break, Julie. I've got enough to deal with, with Max and Monty's shots."

Then she said she didn't even have time to breathe and I should get into the bath right now, and before that I should clear up my homework that was spread out all over the house. Also, would I please put my socks in the laundry basket and make sure to keep them together too, otherwise we'd never see them again?

"What is the story with socks? Could someone please explain it to me?" asked Mom. (This was one of her pet peeves.) "You go out and buy a pair of socks.

But the minute you get home, they make a secret deal, and each one goes its own way. While one of them is dancing around with the clothes in the washing machine, the other one decides to hide in a pillowcase and is never seen again. There's actually no such thing as a 'pair of socks,' and anyone who says there is doesn't know what he's talking about." That was what Mom said. She could be really cute sometimes. I just wished she had more patience.

●　●　●

At night, I lay in bed and thought about Shakshuka, and I couldn't sleep because of all the things I kept imagining, and I also felt cold, even though the windows were closed. I sat up and stared hard, straight ahead, like Brody's grandmother, but not at the wall. I was looking at the picture of the angry chicken that was hanging there. And my thoughts went round and round in my head like the ingredients in a food processor when we pour them in to make a cake.

There was that moment when you could still see the flour, the Smertz sugar, the eggs, and even the lemon peel that Mom grated super thin for lemon zest—and then suddenly there was no flour, no eggs, no Smertz sugar, no bits of lemon—it was something new. And that was what happened to me. My thoughts mixed together until they turned into batter. Then I thought that I should go to Danny's house. If he kidnapped Shakshuka, she might be there. I was sure that Brody would come with me.

How could it be that Effie saw Danny and Duke running but she didn't see Shakshuka? And why were they running in the first place? Maybe one of them was holding Shakshuka and Effie just didn't notice.

I snuggled down under the blanket and managed to fall asleep. But I was still cold. Ever since Shakshuka disappeared, I've been shaking and shivering with cold all night long.

CHAPTER 3

We didn't actually adopt Shakshuka. It was more like she adopted us.

Mom was sitting with the twins in the yard of our building, and suddenly we saw her—she was a tiny thing covered with spots and stripes. She wasn't scared at all and she came right up to us and gave Max a kiss in his mouth, and Mom didn't have the heart to push her away. Later we went in the house and she stayed outside, but when Mom started making supper we could hear her barking, telling us that she was hungry too, and Mom told me that if the noise didn't stop, she'd catch that dog, iron it flat, and turn it into a bath mat.

I managed to sneak out some food and then it was

quiet again. In the evening, Dad came home and he made himself some *shakshuka*—that was the name of this recipe for poached eggs in a yummy tomato sauce—and the puppy barked at him too, until he finally gave her some, and that was when we started calling her Shakshuka, and she turned into a real dog, only one without a collar or a proper dog tag. If the dogcatcher found her without a dog tag, he would lock her up because he'd think she was a stray. And if ten days passed and no one came to claim her—never mind. Forget it.

Two days after Shakshuka disappeared I sat in class and tried to draw a picture of her. But how could I? On her left side, she had this kind of light Smertz path that curved between two hill-shaped spots, one gray and one so light gray, it was almost blue. On her right side, she had a big mess of spots and stripes. Her tail was striped all over, and one of her ears was white with a bit of black. I couldn't remember what the other ear looked like.

After school, Brody and I decided to go do some detective work at Danny's house. When the bell rang we packed our stuff and tried to sneak out as quickly as we could, before any of the kids from our neighborhood decided to walk home with us. But Adam, who was standing in the middle of the classroom, explaining to some girls that if you dip a chip in water before you eat it so that it gets all soggy, it will cure your cold—well, it seems he had heard a little too much.

"Where are y-you g-g-going?"

"Nowhere," we said. "Home."

"To look for your d-d-dog?"

"Forget about it, Adam."

Adam said, "Okay. D-d-did you know that I also have a d-d—"

Brody tried to help Adam finish his sentence. "Dinosaur? Doorbell?"

Adam motioned with his hand to make Brody stop, but he wouldn't. "Dragon? Dishwasher? Donkey?"

I grabbed Brody by the sleeve and dragged him away before he could start making donkey noises.

Adam ran after us as far as the classroom door. He wouldn't shut up.

"But mine's a b-boy. I m-mean, he's a m-male."

"That's great, Adam, congratulations," said Brody.

"What? Does he have a new baby brother?" I asked Brody as we rushed through the school gate, surrounded by a bunch of noisy first graders.

"Who?"

"Adam."

"Why would he have a new baby brother?" asked Brody.

"I don't know. Isn't that what he was telling us?"

"H-how sh-sh-should I kn-know what Adam w-was s-s-saying?" said Brody. Brody said mean things, but he never actually did anything mean. Sometimes I didn't understand how that was possible.

Mom was also a bit like that. Last night she was in a pretty good mood for a change and she asked me what I would want to be if I wasn't a girl named Julie. I said I didn't know, and she put her arms around me and said I wasn't a girl named Julie, but a sweet cake made totally out of chocolate. And she gave me a hug and tickled my stomach, as if I was Max or Monty, and she said, "You see? All this is made out of chocolate!"

And then I asked her what she'd like to be if she wasn't Mom, and she thought for a minute and said if she wasn't Mom who worked at the bank and had taken a long time off to stay home with the twins, she'd be an explorer or a sea captain. I tried to imagine her as a sea captain, holding Max in one hand, a pair of binoculars in the other, with a pacifier hanging around her neck, and I thought it was pretty funny.

"But I wouldn't do anything too serious," said

Mom. "I'd let other people sail the ship. I'd just lie on the deck in the sun and drink rum all day long."

"What's rum?"

"It's like wine."

"That's great, Mom."

Mom looked really happy, as if the boat story was really happening. She kissed me in the place between my forehead and my nose, which was her favorite kissing spot, and said, "Now jump into bed. Did you brush your teeth?"

●◉●

There was a high wall around Danny's house and you couldn't get in unless someone opened the gate from the inside. We walked all the way around twice before we saw that we could crawl under the barrier to the parking lot. Danny lived on the first floor, but we didn't see anyone at his house. It was really quiet.

"Maybe I should whistle for Shakshuka," I said to Brody. "If she's inside the house, she may hear me and start barking." When we were next to Danny's window, I just couldn't help it and I started singing:

"Little boy Danny does nothing but cry.
Why? Why? Why?"

And Brody finished it off: "'Cause he's such a creepy guy!"

And then I saw him. He was standing by the open window looking straight at me.

Shoot! How could we forget? He was suspended!

Danny asked, "What are you doing here? Did you come to get back at me?" What was he talking about? He knew I wouldn't dare hit him, especially in his own house.

Danny said, "Looking for a stone, Julie?"

I looked at Brody, but he didn't understand what Danny was talking about either.

"I'm looking for my dog," I said. I noticed that my legs were shaking, but I tried to stand still.

Danny said, "I don't know where your dog is." But he had this knowing smile.

Then my words just tumbled out. "They saw you running from my house. They saw you and Duke."

Danny said, "So what? I didn't do anything."

"You're a liar," I said.

"You're the liar," Danny replied. "Why did you tell Mrs. Brown that I threw the plant?"

I asked him again where my dog was, even though I knew he wouldn't tell me. Then I started whistling for Shakshuka, and I whistled and whistled until there were tears in my eyes, and Brody dragged me away from there because there really wasn't anything else we could do and anyway it had started raining, and I thought about the angry chicken on the wall in my room and I knew that I wouldn't fall asleep that night either.

●　◉　●

I was cold again that night and I asked Mom to turn on the heater, but I was still freezing and I could hear voices through the window that looked onto Brody's apartment.

And then I saw an ambulance pull up next to our house. A couple of people went into Brody's apartment building with a stretcher, and then they came out again. I strained my eyes to see who was lying there, but it was too dark.

But then it wasn't hard to figure out who it was because the person sat up and tried to push everyone away and get off the stretcher and I could tell it was Brody's grandmother. I could hear her telling them that she knew they listened to her all the time through the pipes, and asking if they were after her jewelry too, and she even slapped one of the people who were trying to calm her down.

What was I thinking about after they took away

Brody's grandmother and it was quiet again? About Danny and his annoying smile; and about this monster-creature I once saw in a cartoon that would get bigger and bigger every time it came up with a new way to take over the world; and about my hair, which only came to my shoulders now; and about Samson the great strongman, who lost his strength after they cut off his hair.

When I finally fell asleep, I dreamed that my mother's food processor was making a really loud noise but nothing was getting mixed together. No matter how hard the machine worked, the ingredients for the cake wouldn't turn into batter.

CHAPTER 4

Brody didn't come to school the next day. I guess no one in his family slept too well that night. I didn't think anyone in the whole building slept well. Anyone except for Mom, who had finally managed to get the Munchkins to sleep after quite a few sleepless nights.

She laid them down, one on each side of her, in my parents' big bed and then went to sleep in the middle, with pillows all around them so they wouldn't roll off. Mom said that if you slept next to a baby, you woke up a little bit healthier. I woke up a little bit healthier after the nights I let Shakshuka sleep in my bed, but Mom didn't know about that because I didn't tell her because she never would have let me.

I felt weird at school, as if the food processor from my dream was still working in my head and making noise. I could barely concentrate in class. And since Brody didn't come to school, I had to hang out with Effie at recess. After a sleepless night, I finally understood what it meant to be Effie—I was so tired I felt completely spaced out. To wake myself up, I helped her organize her schoolbag after a carton of chocolate milk exploded inside it. I thought she'd been carrying it around for about two weeks.

Then we sat on the bench beside the water fountain and tried not to listen to Adam, who was standing nearby driving a bunch of girls crazy with his stories. We were sure he was telling the one about how he was born on a plane on the way to Antarctica, and how the moment the plane landed they came out and covered him with about twenty coats made of polar-bear fur. But Adam was full of surprises, and what he actually said was that yesterday—for real!—he ate a chocolate-coated cookie and found a cockroach in it, and it was chocolate-coated too! All the girls laughed and Adam looked really pleased with himself, but I wasn't sure he should have felt so good. And then I thought, well, at least when they laughed at him, they were paying attention to him. But nobody ever noticed Effie.

When Effie and I walked away from Adam and the

girls, we passed by Danny and Duke. Danny pretended to pick up a stone and throw it at me, but I ignored him. "Danny is so lame," I told Effie. "Mrs. Brown's standing and talking to the pregnant substitute gym teacher really close to him and he's thinking about throwing a stone at me. If you're going to be a jerk, you should at least be smart enough not to get into trouble."

Effie didn't answer me, and then I noticed she was staring at the pregnant substitute gym teacher, who looked as if she was going to have her baby in about fifteen seconds. "Hey, why is she so fat?" Effie asked after a long pause. "It looks like she swallowed the boys' football."

"Yeah, right, that's exactly what happened. And now the ball's growing bigger and bigger in her stomach. Don't ask what'll come out of there in the end!" I said as I dragged her away. Effie was the most spaced-out person I'd ever met. I didn't know how she didn't just float away.

● ● ●

In the afternoon, I went up to Brody's apartment, but there were lots of people there because of what happened with his grandmother, so I turned right around to go back home, but Brody's sister, Nina, grabbed me and pulled me inside.

We rushed past the million and a half people standing around in the living room and went out onto the balcony, where I saw Brody sitting beside his grandmother. He looked very serious, and I noticed that he was holding her hand. I'd never seen him like that with her. Usually he just waited for her to say something so he could laugh at her. Later, he told me that the doctors wanted to send her off to an old-age home, but he and Nina wouldn't let them. In the meantime, they'd changed her medication and she was back at home.

When Brody's grandmother saw me, her eyes got even bigger and rounder and she asked Brody, "Who's the mademoiselle?"

"She's a girl from my class," he said.

Brody's grandmother looked at me as if she didn't really believe Brody, and then she said, "The most important thing, dear, is that you take care of yourself. And don't go walking outside alone because terrible things happen around here. You could get kidnapped from here, from right out front in the yard."

"I know," I answered without thinking twice. "That's what happened to my dog."

Brody poked me with his elbow to tell me to shut

up, but it was too late. Brody's grandmother got all excited, probably because for once someone was agreeing with her, and she started telling me about how she was sitting on the balcony a few days before when she saw two thieves, and how those thieves threw a stone at a downstairs window.

"And even after I screamed and scared them away," said Brody's grandmother, "everyone said that it didn't really happen. They said I'd seen it on TV. But I wasn't sitting in front of the television when it happened. I was sitting on the balcony! Right here!"

I listened to her, and slowly I realized that she wasn't making it up. This was one story that I knew for sure she wasn't making up, and I didn't care that Brody was sitting there making bored faces.

Suddenly the yard in front of our building did seem like a scary place. It wasn't only that dogs and grandmothers got kidnapped there, but other bad things happened there as well. For a moment I could even imagine the people eavesdropping on Brody's grandmother through the pipes in the walls, but I quickly dropped that thought because I realized it really didn't make sense.

I couldn't remember what else Brody's grandmother said. I thought she was trying to convince us that the nice people on TV would never throw stones at windows. Then I quickly went into the living room and I may even have pushed aside a few people who were in my way, and then I ran down the stairs. I knew that Brody had seen the look on my face and that he would be worried, and I knew that he'd follow me in a minute to see what had happened, but I didn't stop to wait for him.

I went into our apartment and jumped over Monty, who was lying on the floor by the door chewing on Mom's mobile phone, and I flew into my room and pulled back the curtain. Now I could see that the window really was broken, and there was glass all over the floor. I wondered how I'd managed not to step on it last night when I was standing near the window watching Brody's grandmother being carried away on the stretcher. Was it because it was too dark?

When Brody came into my room, I showed him the glass.

"Why did you take off like that?" he asked.

"Haven't you figured it out yet?" I said to him.

"No," he said. "What's there to figure out?"

"You're even dumber than you look," I said. "This is glass. My window's broken."

"That's great," said Brody. "Do you have any other broken things you'd like to show me today?"

"Listen to me, you celery head. Your grandmother

said that a couple of days ago there were thieves here and they threw a stone at a window. It was my window. Don't you see what that means?"

"It means my grandmother didn't make it up," said Brody after thinking about it for a minute. "Which is very nice because it must be the first time in twenty years that she hasn't talked nonsense."

"But who threw the stone, dimwit?" I was so excited, I couldn't stop calling him names. "Danny and Duke! They were here and they threw the stone at my window, and then your grandmother heard the noise and started shouting, 'Thieves! Thieves!' and they ran away. That's why Effie saw them running like crazy on the street."

"But where's Shakshuka?" asked Brody.

"I don't know," I said, and by accident I cut myself. It was just a little cut, with the piece of broken glass I was holding.

"Maybe she ran after them," said Brody.

"Yeah, she does that. She loves people who run really fast."

"Listen," said Brody. "They didn't mean to kidnap Shakshuka. They just wanted to break your window for revenge. But when they saw Shakshuka, they whistled and she followed them."

"It all fits!" I said. "Fact: Ever since Shakshuka

disappeared, I'm cold at night. So Shakshuka must have disappeared the night they threw the stone at my window."

"And another thing!" Brody shouted, getting more and more excited. "Remember when we went to Danny's house and he asked if you came to get back at him?"

"Sure," I said.

"He thought you wanted to break his window, just like he'd broken yours. He even asked if you were looking for a stone, remember?"

I sat on the edge of my chair and sucked my finger, which was still bleeding a little.

"We're geniuses!" said Brody. "But where's the dog? And what's a 'celery head'?"

CHAPTER 5

The morning started off really badly. Danny and Duke were making trouble even before the bell rang. They pushed lots of kids and Effie fell down.

They always did things like that, as if it was by accident, and then they said "Sorry" and burst out laughing. This time they also threw Effie's pencil case on the floor, and I crawled around and picked up the heart-shaped stickers she collects, and a pencil sharpener that was clogged with orange Plasticine, and a little fairy toy that was now covered with white-out that had spilled on it when everything fell out.

I gave Effie the fairy, which was ruined, and I turned to Danny because I could see no one was listening, and said, "I know you broke the window in my room. Brody's grandmother saw you from the balcony."

Danny didn't know what to say, so I went on. "Breaking a window isn't funny. If I tell on you and Brody's grandmother says what she knows, you'll be in big trouble."

Danny didn't know that Brody's grandmother was a little confused and she might not have been able to say exactly who threw the stone, and that no one ever believed her anyway.

He whispered so the other kids wouldn't hear, and he said that he and Duke really did come to my house and that they did throw a stone at my window, and then this old lady started shouting 'Thieves! Thieves!' and they ran away. He said there really was a small dog that ran after them, a spotted dog. They whistled to her and she ran after them for a while, but then she disappeared.

I knew he wouldn't tell me more, but I wouldn't give up. "Tell me what happened to her or I'll tell on you."

"You said you wouldn't tell on me if I told you what happened, right? So that's it. I told you what happened. Now move."

I wouldn't move, and Danny pushed me. Suddenly Effie said, "Leave her alone, Danny."

Danny wasn't used to hearing Effie talk. Actually, no one was used to hearing her talk, but after a moment he decided that it wasn't such a big deal and he pushed me again. "I won't leave her alone," he said to Effie. "So what's going to happen to me?"

Nothing will happen to you, I thought. You're Danny plus Duke. But then Effie moved super fast, using one of her karate moves as if she had four hands, and before he could react, Danny found himself sitting on the floor. She really liked that fairy, and maybe she also decided to stick up for me, and those Vietnamese Martial Arts classes she'd been taking finally came in handy.

When Mrs. Brown walked into the class—she always knew just when to show up—Brody told her that Effie was showing us how to do cartwheels. "It's my fault," he said. "I asked her to do that. She just didn't notice Danny standing there and she accidentally bumped into him.

"It's not a big deal," Brody went on. "Danny has knocked down Effie by accident so many times, and this time she accidentally knocked him down."

Everyone smiled, and I thought that sometimes good things could come out of Brody's big mouth, but Mrs. Brown said that she wouldn't put up with violence, even if the whole class stood by the kid who did the hitting. She went over to Danny and helped him up and asked him if Effie had hit him.

"Are you for real?" Danny said, and he tried to send a sneering look in Effie's direction. "The floor was slippery or something. Someone spilled some white-out."

"That's not true," said Effie.

Effie was in seventh heaven because of the note she took home that day, a genuine letter addressed to her parents saying that their daughter had hit another child, and not just any child, but Danny.

At recess and after school, all the little kids pointed at Effie and said that not only was she the fastest in her whole grade, but she beat up boys too.

It was only much later, when we were leaving school one day, that Effie told me that she didn't really mean to do it. It just happened. And the only thing she could think about was how good it would feel to knock Danny down.

"And afterward I was really angry with myself because in martial arts you're not allowed to lose control," Effie said.

"Never mind," I told her. "Think about Danny. He always loses control, and he never feels bad about it."

"Yeah, I know a lot of kids got all excited about it," said Effie. "But I didn't. Hey, what happened to the plant?" We walked out of school and stopped by the pipe where the water always dripped. All the other kids had already forgotten that a plant had ever been there, but Effie had only just noticed it was missing.

I looked around carefully to make sure no one could hear us, and I said, "I threw it at Danny, but don't tell anyone."

"Too bad," said Effie. "It was a nice plant."

And I remembered how I threw the plant at Danny, and how I lied and blamed him and everyone believed me. And then I butted Effie's shoulder softly with my head. Why did we love Effie? Because with all her speed and all her strength, she was just as innocent as my baby brothers were. She was like a pretty plant in a pot, and she could never tell a lie.

◦ ◉ ◦

The day that started with Effie's fairy getting wrecked, the day when Effie knocked down Danny and went home with a note for her parents, ended in the vegetable patch. Brody and I were pulling up weeds when he said, "Before, you had something to hope for because you thought Danny knew something. But now it's the worst. You know that you don't know anything."

Then he said, "Maybe the dogcatcher really did get her."

And then he said, "The more time passes, the less chance there is of finding her. That's what the police always say when people disappear."

I said, "Okay, enough."

"Maybe she got run over by a car," Brody said, pulling up a plant.

"That's a lettuce, not a weed, lamebrain," I said, and I pushed him.

Brody got angry. "Why are you pushing me?"

I didn't answer him. I just went over and sat down on the side, on the chair with the crooked leg—the one that looked like it had rotted in the rain.

I pretended I was fixing the straps on my sport shoes, and I could hear Adam telling another one of his stories about how when he took the dog out for a walk last night he passed by the air-conditioner factory and there was a robbery going on, so he called the police on his mobile phone, and before the police arrived he heard gunshots from inside because the security guard must have found the burglars and they were probably trying to get away.

Nobody believed Adam because everyone remembered how he once caught a burglar who was trying to climb in his bedroom window but it turned out that the burglar was just a guy who came to fix the shutters. But this story was a pretty good one, and he managed to tell it without stuttering too much, so in the end the whole class listened to him, except for Danny and Duke, who were busy punching each other.

I was also sort of listening, and at the same time I was using my foot to draw a big rectangle on the ground, which was supposed to be the air-conditioner factory. Then I tried imagining where Adam was standing and where the burglars were, and I knew there was something else about this fairy tale that I should be paying attention to, but what could possibly be important in another one of Adam's made-up stories?

In the meantime, the bell rang and everyone went home, and Brody went too, and only I kept on sitting there on the rotten chair, thinking about how if someone disappeared forever, bit by bit you started to forget all about her. That was the rule. If I didn't manage to find Shakshuka, all her spots and stripes would slowly be erased from my memory like the numbers in math class were erased from the board.

Suddenly I realized that Danny was sitting next to one of the flower boxes, putting on his torn sneakers. "I don't care about you breaking my window. I only care about my dog," I said to him as if he was my friend, as if he cared about me, as if he cared about a little dog that hadn't eaten in four days and was maybe tied to a tree somewhere, or wandering the streets, or worse.

"I really don't know where she is," said Danny. He sounded almost nice when he said that.

I just sat there for a little longer, and then I figured it out. Why didn't I think of this before? I was at the gate in a flash asking everyone where Adam was, but he'd already gone. Luckily, Brody was still there, and I told him we had to get to Adam right away.

We ran two blocks until we caught up with him. "Adam! Adam!" I shouted. "What color is your dog?"

Adam looked scared. He turned as white as a sheet of paper, as white as a first grader who bumped into Danny behind the nature teacher's greenhouse.

"You said you were taking your dog for a walk past the air-conditioner factory when you caught the burglars. Since when do you have a dog? And what color is it?"

"All s-sorts of c-c-colors," said Adam, who seemed to be stuttering more than usual.

"A little one? That likes to jump?"

Adam looked as if he was about to burst into tears.

"Right, on one side it looks like there's a path drawn on her, with two hills? And her tail is all striped? And one ear is white with a bit of black?"

Adam said he didn't remember exactly. He only remembered that a few days ago he saw a little puppy near his house and he fell in love with it, and he put some blankets in a cardboard box from the super in the basement of his building so it would have somewhere to sleep, and he didn't tell his parents because they'd never let him keep it.

Since then, every day, first thing in the morning and right after school (and once before bedtime), he had brought the puppy food and taken it for a walk with a leash. And he really, really didn't think it was my Shakshuka. He thought it was a boy dog.

Adam stuttered pretty fast but talked very slowly. It took him a long time to get the whole story out. While he was talking, we walked him home, and then there we were, outside the basement door, and the door opened and I saw her and I was afraid that it wasn't really her, but then I felt her tongue licking my cheek and I wanted to hug her, but there was no chance because she wouldn't stop jumping.

I touched her and thought, It's her, it's really her, and I was still scared that in a second I'd wake up and discover it was all a dream, but then I realized that a dream didn't bark and didn't lick your face, and I started crying like a baby even though Brody and Adam were right there. I could hear myself and I couldn't believe it. I sounded just like my baby brothers. And Shakshuka was howling too.

"*Now* you're crying?" said Brody. "What are you crying for? You've found her!"

I wasn't listening to him because I was too busy trying to hold Shakshuka still so I could look her in the eyes and tell her that she was the stupidest, ugliest dog in the world, and Brody told Adam that was how I always talked when I got emotional.

The first thing I did was check her other ear, the one I couldn't remember. It was bluish-gray. Some kids might have thought that wasn't important, but those kids had probably never seen a dog with such an amazing coat. Those kids probably thought that all dogs were the same.

I used to be like that too, actually. Before the Munchkins were born I was sure that all babies were the same. That they all cried and spit up and there was no difference between them. But now I could tell with my eyes closed which of the twins woke up first in the morning and started babbling.

Just as we got to the entrance of the building, Brody and Shakshuka and I, Effie came back from her Underwater Pottery class and saw us. She stopped and held her head in her hands and said, "I don't believe it!"

"Believe it, believe it," I said as I stroked Shakshuka.

"You got a haircut!" said Effie.

Brody and I gave each other a look.

"Two weeks ago . . . maybe more," I told her.

"It suits you. It's a new look," said Effie.

What could I say? I said thanks, and I really did feel brand-new.

That night I spent a long time looking at the angry chicken hanging on my wall and I thought that maybe there really were people eavesdropping through the pipes in our building, like Brody's grandmother said. Why not? Stranger things had happened.

Fact: Danny got mad in computer class and threw a chair at a boy two years younger than us, and the boy actually wasn't badly hurt, but the chair broke and one of its legs went flying through the window and got stuck on the head of the scarecrow that we built in nature class, and now the scarecrow looked like an alien with a horn.

And another fact: The police really did invite Adam to a special ceremony—Mrs. Brown even told us in class—because he really did hear gunshots and called the police when he was walking past the air-conditioner factory with Shakshuka, and that was how they caught the burglars and now he was going to get, Brody said, a cer-cer-certificate of m-m-m-merit for his b-b-bravery. I really hoped that it made him feel better about his dog not being his anymore, and about his he-dog really being a she-dog.

And Dad was coming back from his business trip tomorrow. And tonight, at long last, I wouldn't be cold, first, because my bedroom window was fixed, and second, because my striped and spotted dog was going to sleep with me and keep me warm. I even told Mom about it while she was baking cookies, and without even thinking she said that dog would be in serious trouble if she started climbing on beds. She might even end up on a cookie tray with icing sugar on top!

And Max said, "Da!"

SHAKSHUKA
STRIKES AGAIN

CHAPTER 1

It all started when I tried to build a toy for my little brothers, and it got more complicated when Danny decided to annoy my cousin Effie with some dumb tongue twister just when she was training for a race and his stupid woodchuck-chucking made her fall and hurt her knee.

I tried really hard to build that toy. I wanted it to be a present for my twin brothers, Max and Monty. It was supposed to be a smart toy, a wooden block with a music box inside, and the smart part was that every time you shook it, you heard this loud corny music. But it kept falling apart, whether I used ordinary glue or superglue.

As if all that wasn't enough, we had a new principal at our school named Blue Dawn, and she'd decided that everything was going to be different from now on, and she could turn our school into a place where everyone behaved all the time, and whenever she caught two kids fighting she called everyone into the school yard and once we were all there explained that violence was not okay, and she also checked to make sure that everyone was wearing the school uniform.

Last week she managed to spin a whole lecture out of what happened when Danny distracted Effie with his tongue twister. He made her lose her concentration at the exact moment when she was about to take off from the starting line.

It was really too bad she fell and hurt her knee because there was an athletic meet coming up, and we were supposed to send Effie to represent our school. Effie was our fastest runner, she ran even faster than the boys, and this time it was really important that she ran and beat Donna Silver from Pine Way School because Donna Silver said, "That Effie, her legs run fast but her head runs slow." But now Effie was walking around with a bandaged knee and it looked like she didn't stand a chance against Donna Silver, and Blue Dawn the principal said all the kids should learn from what happened to Effie, and they should get up every morning and do a good deed, simple as that, get up and think of something nice to do instead of fighting.

Of all people it was Danny—the kid who speeches like that were invented for—who turned away when he thought no one was looking, his hands in his pockets, and in a loud voice recited the same dumb tongue twister he'd been shouting every day—"How much wood would a woodchuck chuck if a woodchuck could chuck wood?"—so he could block out every word that the principal was saying. That tongue twister had been running through his head because the kids in first grade had been repeating it nonstop for the past few weeks, ever since one of them learned it from his dad, who told him that about a hundred years ago they would say it together on the bus on field trips.

Danny was always hitting kids and annoying them and causing trouble, and it was too bad that of all ears he chose to recite his "woodchuck" right into Effie's, but this time I could understand why he was saying it to himself while the principal was talking. She'd decided to make a good boy out of him, and lately he was getting scared that she might actually succeed.

After school the three of us went to my house to eat—Brody, Effie, and me. Sometimes they came over to eat spaghetti. Mom looked at Effie's knee and told her not to give up on the race. She said she should train every day and in the end it would all work out.

Afterward she told us to be careful because Shakshuka looked like she was getting ready to attack.

Shakshuka was lying under Brody's chair, having a snooze. Effie stared at my mom with big, round eyes, since between races most of the time Effie was pretty spaced out and she hadn't learned yet that you couldn't believe anything my mother said.

"I don't understand how you can raise such a scary animal," Brody said in a pretend-serious voice because he was pretty evil himself, especially when it came to words, and he always got my mom's jokes.

And Mom said, "Really, Julie, you'd better control that wild dog of yours. Do you think we live in a jungle here?"

Shakshuka rolled over and sighed in her sleep. "But the dog is fast asleep," said Effie, who didn't always understand that kind of joke, and she leaned down to get a closer look at Shakshuka, and her hair fell into her soup but she didn't notice. That was Space-Effie for you.

●◐●

After we ate, we went out to play behind our building and Shakshuka came with us and I showed Effie and Brody how you could stroke her fur so that she looked like a princess with her hair tied back, and then Brody had an idea about how to get Effie's knee back in shape for the race, and all we needed was some help from Shakshuka.

Have you ever seen a race between a girl and a dog? It was true that Effie was the fastest runner in the class and that she beat all the boys, but Shakshuka ran like the bravest warrior princess and that was even better. Brody told Shakshuka that if she was smart and took advantage of Effie's injury, she could win, but Shakshuka didn't pay any attention to him.

Just when the race started, she stopped to smell an old tire lying on its side with some weeds growing in the middle, and then she started barking at a cat that was hiding under a car, and Effie won easily.

Brody said we had to try something else, and we thought about it for a long time until we decided that I would stand at the finish line and call Shakshuka, and Brody would hold her at the starting line so she couldn't move, and then he would say "On your mark, get set, go!" and release her, and they would both start running toward me.

"Come on, little one," I called to Shakshuka from far away, while Brody was still holding her. "Come fast."

"Fast isn't enough," Brody said. "You also have to know which way to run."

Shakshuka wriggled in his grasp because she wanted to get to me, and Brody said, "Okay, ready?"

I looked over at Effie and saw she was busy braiding her hair, not paying attention to anything else, and I realized that this was our chance to beat her, so I answered quickly, "Ready."

"Set, go!" said Brody, and he let Shakshuka go, and she ran straight to me like a good girl, and that was how she managed to do what no one in our school had ever dreamed of—she beat Effie.

"I didn't even realize that we were supposed to start running," Effie said, and I knew that was true, and that I could have jolted her out of her daydream, but I didn't do it because it was about time Effie lost for once. Why shouldn't she? She always won.

Brody told her that it was a race, not a space mission, so there was no reason to be spaced out, and I petted Shakshuka and sang:

> *"Blue Dawn may rise and shine,*
> *But the winning dog is mine."*

"But Effie won the first race," Brody said.

"Yes," I said, "but that race doesn't count because Shakshuka barked at a cat."

"No," Brody said, "it's not Effie's fault that your dog barks at cats when she's supposed to run."

"And it's not my dog's fault that Effie falls asleep on her feet," I said.

Brody and I almost got into a fight, but then I noticed that Effie and Shakshuka had started to run around in circles, the two of them with their hair streaming behind their ears, and they both had such happy faces, like they didn't want or need anything, as if running was the best thing in the world.

That was all very nice, I thought, but it couldn't be for real. In a race, there's only one winner.

CHAPTER 2

Everything seemed to be going well. Effie managed to get rid of the bandage on her knee and went back to training, and lots of kids thought she had a good chance of beating Donna Silver from Pine Way School, who was better known as the Jet. Effie saw her once a week in the afternoon when they both practiced the shot put and threw these heavy iron balls, always with their left arms, and the rumor was that at the last practice Donna Silver said that Effie's legs were strong but the rest of her wasn't too impressive, and everyone in our class heard about it and was really angry because we never talked that way about Effie, we all looked out for her, except for Danny, who didn't look out for anyone, but maybe even that was beginning to change these days. I couldn't tell for sure.

Anyway, Effie didn't say anything to Donna Silver because she didn't know how to react to that kind of talk, and it really wasn't her fault that she had legs like that, and Brody said he was sure that Effie would win easily because Donna Silver may have been a jet, but Effie was a spaceship, and a spaceship was much faster than any jet. Brody said things like that to make fun of Effie, but Effie couldn't care less.

●◉●

Principal Blue Dawn walked into our class a few days before the race and said she would be substituting for our teacher, Mrs. Brown, who came down with the flu, and first of all, she wanted to remind us that in her class gum chewing was forbidden, and absolutely no trading stickers at recess, and she warned us that she would confiscate everything and we would never see it again, simple as that, and mobile phones weren't allowed, and at morning recess we could only have sandwiches and no candy, and we were not allowed to bring balloons onto school property, even if it was our friend's birthday, because it wasn't fair to the kids who didn't get balloons, and you, excuse me, Effie, what is that you're eating in the middle of a lesson?

"Chocolate," said Effie.

We all turned and looked. On Effie's desk there was a giant, double-size chocolate bar with nuts, and Effie answered the principal with her mouth full of chocolate, and even smiled when she noticed that all the kids were looking at her, but then she realized that she was in trouble because Blue Dawn was definitely not Mrs. Brown and she didn't find these kinds of things funny, so she quickly put away the chocolate in her schoolbag and wiped her mouth on her sleeve, and Blue Dawn the principal said, "Give that to me, please."

"But it's mine," Effie said.

"Don't you know that you're not allowed to bring chocolate to school?" asked our principal.

"I didn't bring it," Effie said.

"But you just said it's yours," the principal said.

Effie shrugged. She didn't have anything else to say. The principal didn't know Effie and couldn't guess that she wasn't much of a talker, and to her Effie seemed plain rude, and she informed her that this was the last time she would accept such behavior and next time things would be very unpleasant.

"As if they're pleasant now," whispered Brody, who was sitting in front of me.

Effie couldn't explain how the chocolate came to be on her desk. Apparently it just appeared there. Adam said that things like that really happened, and he even read once in some book about a girl who had chocolate bars materialize in her pockets. "And sometimes," Adam said, "wh-wh-when she wore clothes with especially big p-p-pockets, whole b-b-b-boxes of chocolates would just g-g-grow there."

I could see that Brody really wanted to imitate Adam and play around with p-p-pockets full of b-b-b-boxes, but Adam was already on his next story, this time about a gardener in Belgium who managed to grow pink eggplant that smelled and tasted like strawberries, and everyone in town thought that was fantastic, but then they discovered that whoever ate them couldn't stop petting cats, and people quit their jobs, forgot about everything else, and spent all their time chasing any cat they could find so they could cuddle it, and in the end the government decided to destroy all the pink eggplant, but when they got to the field they saw that a pack of wild boars had already scarfed down the whole lot—

I dragged Effie away from there. As usual she was

standing and listening, her mouth slightly open, her wide eyes unblinking, as if Adam's crazy talk was the most interesting thing she had ever heard in her life. "Beware the mighty Blue Dawn," I told her.

"Fine," said Effie, but she wasn't listening, and a minute later she asked, "Beware the what? Why should I be afraid of her?"

"Because she can make our lives difficult," I said. "Let's hope Danny's afraid of her too and starts acting like a good kid."

Danny was coming toward us. Right beside him, as always, was Duke, his loyal number two. When Danny reached us, I quickly moved in between him and Effie so he couldn't get to her. But Danny only mumbled, "How much wood would a woodchuck chuck," and looked at us with a little grin on his face, and when Duke finished off "If a woodchuck could chuck wood," Danny jabbed him with his elbow so he'd keep quiet. Danny sometimes had these nice moments, but it didn't happen often, and you could never tell if those moments were the real thing and all the rest was just an act to impress his friends, or if it was the other way round.

Effie didn't pay any attention to Danny, just like she didn't really pay attention to Blue Dawn, and for once they left us alone. I asked her if it was true that she didn't know who had given her the chocolate, and she said she had no idea. There was a scrap of paper on her desk but nothing was written on it; there were just some scribbles she couldn't read properly, so she threw it away along with the chocolate wrapper.

We went out to the school yard and played hopscotch, and after that we jumped rope with some other girls and it was fun, and then Effie remembered Adam's story and asked me what would happen to the cats now, after the wild boars had eaten all the pink eggplant. The poor kitties.

And on the far fence, the one next to the nature teacher's greenhouse, a big black cat was moving its tail just above the rhyme that someone had written in chalk:

> Principal Dawn
> Has a hole in her shoe.
> You can see right through.
> And her stockings are blue!

CHAPTER 3

In the evening, after I showed Dad how to brush Shakshuka so she looked like the most gorgeous princess, I asked him what to do about the toy I was building for Max and Monty. I wanted it to be a perfect wooden cube with a ball inside that played music when you shook it. At our last woodworking class, it actually looked pretty good.

I used a hot-glue gun to stick the sides together and left it to dry, but when I tried to shake it, it fell apart again and the musical ball came flying out.

Dad suggested using a hammer and nails so that it would hold together better, but Monty was getting a little too interested in the hammer, so I put it in my schoolbag really fast, and then I gave him a big kiss on the forehead so he wouldn't feel bad. Monty was interested in everything except for kisses. When he crawled past Shakshuka, he lifted up her ear and tried to peek inside. When you gave him a baby bottle, he sometimes managed to twist off the top and open it and turn it upside down so that everything spilled all over the floor. And if he got his hands on one of my notebooks, he destroyed it in a second. Max was actually very interested in kisses. And when he really liked me, he pulled my hair, and I let him.

In the morning the two of them came to wake me up, and Max crawled under my covers and said, "Up, Julie, up," and Monty sat on the floor and checked what happened when you put your hand in a cup of water, and tried to figure out why in the end the water always spilled, and I got up quickly because I wanted to be the first one in class to see if more chocolate would appear on Effie's desk. But this time there were five big balloons, all of them tied to her chair, and on each one was written in block letters: "Effie's the Champ!"

Stuck to her chair was a note that Effie tried to read, but she couldn't make it out and she didn't care anyway. She folded it into a paper airplane, and Brody laughed and said that Effie's airplane looked like a spaceship, but Effie didn't mind about that either. She loved those balloons, you could see it on her face, and she even got up on a table and did a headstand, which was really something that didn't happen every day.

When Mrs. Brown walked into the classroom, Brody explained to her that even though everyone knew balloons weren't allowed at school, this was a special case and that should be taken into consideration.

"A special case?" said Mrs. Brown, laughing as Effie sat down looking like a queen on her throne and above her head in every direction floated the words Effie's the Champ!, Effie's the Champ!, Effie's the Champ!, Effie's the Champ!, Effie's the Champ! on five balloons.

"Extra-special," Brody said. He was good at that kind of talk. "She was injured, her knee was in bad shape, but now she's back to training and she can run in the race. We have to keep her happy, you know."

Mrs. Brown knew. Everyone understood. At recess kids came from the other classes to see the balloons and everyone thought they were great, and no one paid any attention to Danny and Duke, who tried to put up a barrier by the door and charge the kids for looking at the balloons.

●　●　●

At the end of the day we had free time and everyone went out to the school yard, except for Effie—who stayed to guard her balloons and draw in her notebook—and me and a few other kids. Danny sat on his desk, drumming with his pencil on an empty plastic bottle, and Duke sat next to him, staring into space.

"Why do you two always have to make so much noise?" I asked Danny. "Could you maybe stop doing that?"

"Could you maybe stop doing that?" Danny said to Duke, trying to sound like me.

Duke just rolled his eyes. When it came to keeping quiet, he was even worse than Effie.

I asked Danny why they weren't outside in the school yard, and he said he'd had enough of the principal, she always managed to find him, and she had this thing she did that was meant to stop fights before they even got started, when she put a heavy hand on your shoulder, and all you wanted to do was escape from that hand, and that was why he would sometimes rather stay in the classroom, even at recess.

I took the pencil from Danny and started to drum on the bottle, and Danny said I couldn't keep the beat, and I said it wasn't possible to mess up the beat with a pencil and a bottle, and then the bell rang and Brody came in and said to Effie, "If you want to take those balloons home, you'd better come now. I heard that the principal left early."

Effie, who was rocking back and forth on her chair, almost flipped over. I tossed the pencil to Danny and said, "Let's go."

We walked fast, and when we passed the blue door of the teachers' room, Brody imitated the principal and said in a mock-serious voice:

"Dawn's door won't let evil through
Because it's painted a lovely blue."

As Effie, Brody, and I were leaving the building, we saw the principal standing by the gate, talking to some of the parents.

Brody and I pushed Effie and her balloons back into the building. "She's standing there so the parents will think she's so nice and be impressed because she pats the little kids on their heads," Brody said, "but what she really wants is to catch the kids who aren't wearing the school uniform."

We told Effie that she couldn't walk out with the balloons because the principal would take them away, and that she had to get rid of them, but there was no way Effie was going to let go of those five promises of success. How could she just give up those balloons, with "Effie's the Champ!" written all over them, even before she had actually won the race? Who cared if almost all the air had already leaked out of one of them? I saw she was holding on to the strings really tightly, and I said, "Let's go. Maybe Blue Dawn won't want to grab the balloons in front of those moms."

But at that exact minute the two mothers who were standing and talking to the principal said goodbye and left, as if all at once everyone had been ordered to leave, and the school yard was empty. As we drew nearer to the principal, who was standing alone by the gate, I felt as if my toes wanted to escape from my shoes, and I tried to calm down by repeating, like Danny, "How much wood would a woodchuck chuck . . ." But it didn't help.

Blue Dawn the principal stopped us as we walked by. "Effie, do I need to congratulate you on winning the race?"

"The r-r-race hasn't even happened yet . . . ," Effie stammered.

"And at this rate, there may not be a race," the principal said. "If this is the way you behave, you can't represent the school. You're not allowed to bring balloons to school."

"Someone gave them to her," Brody said.

"Apparently whoever gave them to her doesn't want her to compete. What's this—'Champ, Champ, Champ'? Let's make sure we're being humble, especially since the race hasn't happened yet."

Effie stood there silently holding the balloons. She was actually very modest, and she was my cousin. I had to think of a way to help her. "It's not her fault," I said.

"Is that so? Then she'd better hand over those balloons this instant. Simple as that."

"But they're mine," Effie said.

I hoped the principal wouldn't punish Effie for answering back because Effie wasn't rude at all, she just said whatever was on her mind and she didn't think first. And I thought that in that way she was a bit like my brothers and Shakshuka, but then I remembered that Shakshuka and the twins didn't know how to talk, and I remembered that my mom was one of those parents who thought that Blue Dawn was a good principal, and thanks to her there was less fighting and things ran more smoothly, and I knew she would agree with Blue Dawn about the balloons because we did need rules and that was just the way it was.

Even though I was deep in thought, I noticed Effie move, raising the hand that was holding the balloons. Everyone looked up. The sky was its usual blue, like always, and gradually I realized what all of us were thinking at that minute, and just then Effie sighed and handed over the balloons to the principal.

On the way home, Brody said to Effie, "It's good that you didn't let go of the balloons because if you had, she wouldn't have let you run in the race." Effie didn't say anything, she just opened and closed her fist, as if her hand was practicing the move that would have released her balloons into the clear blue sky, where they would have disappeared and not belonged to anyone.

"The air would have leaked out pretty soon, anyway," Brody said, and I told him to shut up, but it was too late, Effie had already started walking really fast. I ran after her and tried to make her feel better about the principal's punishment—no recess tomorrow—and I told her it was no big deal, she could train inside as well, and we would all move the desks out of the way for her.

Effie didn't say a word, so I asked her if she knew that my brother Max liked to sleep with a ratty old purple blanket.

It seemed to me that she nodded yes, so I kept on, telling her about how when you put Max to sleep you had to make sure the blanket was all the way over his head or he got angry, so Mom always covered his head and gave him these "power pats"—pats on the back that were so strong they made his whole body move— and she laughed and told him that he was right, life was hard, but you had to know what to take to heart and what not to. And then he tried to fall asleep and he tossed and turned and the blanket fell off, and he got upset, and Mom came back and stroked him and explained that you could never win when you were battling a blanket, it was a lost cause, the baby hadn't been born yet who could convince a blanket to do something it didn't feel like doing.

"Why are you telling her about that?" asked Brody, who had managed to catch up with us.

"Because . . . ," I started to explain. "Because I just . . ."

"I'll tell you why," he said. "It's because Blue Dawn is like that blanket. You can never win when she's around."

Effie almost smiled, almost, and I was so happy, I butted her shoulder with my head, but not too hard.

In the afternoon, Effie came back from her shot put practice and refused to say a word about Donna Silver. She just ran round and round the building, try-

ing to calm down. Brody and I sat on the steps and petted Shakshuka, and Brody said he'd like to know who brought Effie the balloons and the chocolate. We thought about lots of different kids, but we couldn't guess who it might have been. For a minute I even suspected Brody, and just to annoy him I said, "But you aren't nice enough to do something like that."

"Maybe it's Adam?" Brody said. "Adam's the kind of kid who's always coming up with funny ideas."

"True," I said, "but he can't keep his mouth shut. If he had brought those balloons to school, we'd all have heard about it by now."

"I know!" Brody said. "It's Donna Silver."

"You think Donna Silver would send Effie balloo that say 'Effie's the Champ!'?" I asked him. "You (be sure that she wants to be the champ herself."

CHAPTER 4

The day before the race, Effie couldn't concentrate on anything. Even on ordinary days, she has trouble concentrating, but now she couldn't focus at all. In woodworking class, she sat on the floor in the corner playing with marbles, and I built a wall of chairs and schoolbags around her so the teacher wouldn't see. The best thing was that I finally managed to build my musical toy. I used Dad's hammer and nails, and I made sure that the points of the nails didn't stick out anywhere because that would be very dangerous for babies.

I kept shaking the cube, and the musical ball inside kept playing its silly music, and the kids shouted at me to stop because it really was an annoying sound, and

in the end I put it away in my bag. But when class was over and I checked to see if it was there, I couldn't find it, even after I turned my bag upside down and looked under all the desks to see if it had fallen out and rolled away. I asked some of the kids, but it was no use. The toy had vanished.

Mom said that on a bad day the best thing to do was to crawl under the covers and go back to sleep and not come out again till morning. But there weren't any beds at school. At recess, when I was walking into the classroom, Danny blocked my way and pushed me. I went flying and almost fell, and I really felt like throwing something at him, but when I got closer I saw that Duke and some other boys had stretched a string between two chairs at the entrance to the room, and I realized that Danny had pushed me to the side so I wouldn't trip over it. I saw that he was untying the string himself, but I still told him that he was stupid.

Before I had even managed to sit down, they told us that the next class was canceled, and that we should line up in pairs and go outside to the school yard quietly because the principal was going to give us one of her character-building lectures. Someone had probably hit someone, so we were going to have to listen to another speech about how instead of fighting, we should get up every morning and think about good deeds and just do them, simple as that. I stood next to Effie and Brody and I was hot and I thought about the toy I made that had just disappeared, simple as that.

And then Effie took off her backpack and threw it on the ground. I didn't understand why she had brought it with her. All the other kids left their school-bags in the classrooms. But Space-Effie had lugged her bag outside, and suddenly it felt heavy, so she threw it down—and from inside it came the sound of the loud, corny music that I knew so well.

Great! I thought. My toy! That's where it got to.

When Effie heard the music she panicked and stared straight at Blue Dawn. More than three hundred kids and teachers, and also Blue Dawn, who was in the middle of a sentence, fell silent.

Effie quickly bent down and grabbed her bag, which was the same one I had, but the music kept on playing. Everyone heard the principal loud and clear through the speakers when she said, "I see that we're still busy getting ready for the race."

Effie was too frightened to move or speak. She just stood there staring at the principal. She looked exactly the way Shakshuka does when Mom catches her sneaking cheese from the table.

"This race," said the principal, "is not compulsory. You don't have to participate. Simple as that."

"It wasn't her, it was me. I put it in her bag," I said because I knew that this time it would be terrible if the principal punished Effie. And to make things crystal clear, I grabbed the bag, took out the wooden cube, and said in a loud voice, "It's mine."

* ● *

No kid liked the principal's office. The principal's office wasn't always punishments and threats, but it was always a dangerous place, and there were always eyes in there that stared at kids, and it didn't matter what kind of kids they were, those eyes made them feel as though they shouldn't be in that room. All the kids I knew wouldn't go near the principal's office unless they didn't have a choice. Danny spent a lot of time in there because whenever he hit someone, he and his parents received an invitation to the principal's office. But Danny wasn't a good example because he wasn't afraid of anything.

I wasn't like Danny. I sat next to the window in the outer office near the principal's room, waiting for my talk with Blue Dawn, and I wanted to disappear into one of the desk drawers, to flatten myself between the pages of the blue calendar on the table, to slip inside the copy machine that was busy spitting out work sheets, and more than anything I wanted to be at home, in bed, running my hand through Shakshuka's fur.

The window was open a crack, and I saw Adam's blond hair as he was about to pass by outside. When he noticed me, I put a finger to my lips, and we started whispering. Adam told me he knew of a way to hypnotize the principal so she wouldn't punish kids. All you had to do was take a pencil and move it slowly from side to side in front of her so that she would start to follow it with her eyes, and in a calm and quiet voice tell her exactly what you wanted her to do. For example, you could say that from today, recess would start at nine and end at noon.

I asked Adam if he had any better ideas.

"They're mad at you," he said.

"Ah," I said. I didn't have the energy to say more than that.

"B-B-Brody and Effie think you b-b-brought the b-b-b-balloons and . . ."

"And the chocolate," I said.

Adam said, "And b-b-b-because of that, the p-p-p-principal is m-m . . ."

"Mad. Because of me the principal is mad at Effie," I said.

Then Blue Dawn the principal arrived—Adam melted away the minute he saw her—and when we were both sitting in her office, she asked me if Effie was my cousin.

"Yes," I replied.

"Why did you give her all those presents at school?" The principal came and sat next to me, and I could feel how my feet wanted to leave my shoes behind and run home. I tried to think of an answer that would keep Effie out of trouble.

"She has to race tomorrow," I said. "She has a good chance. No other girl can run like her, not even Donna Silver from Pine Way School. Effie can even beat my dog."

"And *I* think," said Principal Blue Dawn in her most wise and solemn voice, "that maybe it's not easy for you to watch your cousin winning trophies. Simple as that."

"No, of course not . . . ," I said, but then I stopped. Maybe I had hurt Effie in some way. After all, I wanted Shakshuka to beat her in that race.

"Jealousy is a tough thing," the principal said.

● ◉ ●

Later, when I told Effie that I must have put the toy in her bag instead of mine by mistake, and that the chocolate and the balloons were not presents from me, and that I didn't mean to get her into trouble with the principal, she didn't say anything at all.

Even whenever everything was okay, Effie hardly said anything, everybody knew that, but when Effie was mad she was quiet in a super-silent way. She kept quiet like keeping quiet was another sport she did really well.

I told Brody, "You know it isn't me. If it was me, you would've seen me carrying the balloons to school. You can't hide balloons in your schoolbag."

"So how did your toy get into Effie's bag?" he asked.

Before I could answer, Danny started circling around me with his "How much wood would a woodchuck chuck . . . ," and I had to chase him away. And then it was the end of the day and that was it, everyone went home and talked about how it was really me who brought Effie the presents but wouldn't admit it, and how it was my fault that the principal was after her, and everyone was sure that I had really gone too far.

CHAPTER 5

When I got home from school, I couldn't sit still. I stared out the window at Effie's building across the street and I knew that right then she was Jumping Rope While Walking Backward and Keeping Balance on a Tightrope Suspended Ten Feet in the Air, and straight from there she would go to Challenge Knitting with Barbed Wire. I'm not exaggerating! These were her afternoon classes. I knew that in the evening she would come home and run around our building five times really fast to make sure she was in shape for the race tomorrow, and I kept thinking about how she wasn't talking to me and how annoying it was that everyone was always watching out for that Effie, that princess, so nothing bad would ever happen to her and her feelings wouldn't get hurt. Of all the kids, she was the one they watched out for—with all her muscles and her strength. Max climbed up on me and pulled my hair really hard, the way he liked to, and it hurt but I barely noticed.

After that Mom yelled at me because my room looked like a winter wonderland, covered with snow, with bits of torn white paper on every surface, and I yelled back that she should ask Monty what happened to the new notebook that he snatched from my desk that morning, and Mom brought a broom and cleaned up the mess but she still made a face, even though this time it wasn't my fault.

"You're the one who's always saying we have to know which things to take to heart," I reminded her, but I could tell she was too tired to listen.

At bedtime I told her that only little kids could ever be happy. Then they got a bit older and went to school and that was when the trouble started. Later they turned into adults like her and Dad and suddenly they had little kids of their own and then they got annoyed all the time. Mom was rocking Max in her arms to help him fall asleep and she said, "So what you're really saying is that only babies are happy people."

"Yes," I said angrily. "Only babies are happy people." And then I thought of Effie.

Mom didn't try to convince me that everything was going to be okay. She didn't say, "Of course grown-ups also know how to be happy." She just looked at me and didn't say a word. Then she hugged me real close and said I belonged to her and she belonged to me and that was the way it would always be, nothing would ever change that.

● ● ●

When I fell asleep that night, I dreamed that I was floating high in the sky, holding on to the string of a balloon. All around me I saw the color blue, the ordinary blue of the sky, and below me was a white cloud, like the kind you see in a cartoon. I heard a dog barking, and I knew it was Shakshuka calling to me from inside the cloud, and I knew that if I let go of the string, I would fall into the cloud and it would be as soft and fluffy as a marshmallow. But even in my dream I knew that you couldn't trust cartoons, and I was afraid to let go of the balloon. When I woke up, I started thinking about Adam, and about what a great storyteller he was. I wasn't sure why. Crazy stories appeared to me only in my dreams, but Adam could come up with a hundred of them every day.

I jumped out of bed, took a new box of colored

chalk from Mom, and rushed to school. During recess I got everyone to make signs, and I asked Adam to draw a big spaceship on each one, and on every spaceship we wrote "Effie's the Champ!" Effie saw what we were doing, of course, and she also heard how everyone was whispering about how she wasn't talking to me. Even Effie couldn't ignore stuff like that, but she still kept quiet. She hardly talked to anyone and just kept doing leg and arm stretches to warm up for the race, and the teacher didn't tell her to stop, even after the bell rang.

The time flew past so fast, as fast as a warrior princess could run, and soon we were on our way to the stadium. On the bus they told us to sit in pairs and they wouldn't let us choose our friends, so it would be easier to keep things under control, and I ended up sitting next to Danny.

"Why is Effie mad at you?" he asked, and he swung his foot as the bus swayed, giving my shoe little kicks.

I didn't feel like talking to him about it. "Because you're stupid," I told him.

"Is that the only insult you know?"

"No. But it's the best one," I said.

Danny didn't say anything, but for the whole ride his shoe kept bumping against mine with those little kicks. Luckily it was a short trip and no one saw.

At the stadium we all sat high above the track and we held up our signs with the spaceships. I could just about tell which runner was Effie by the school shirt she was wearing. And then they blew the whistle and Effie ran.

Obviously it wasn't only Effie who ran. There were lots of girls there. Donna Silver shot out first and it looked as if it would be impossible to catch up with her. Everyone around me was screaming, but I heard only Effie's silence. I mean it, I could hear it, I could hear how silently she ran, and how serious she was, strong and sealed off like a real spaceship, and on the second lap she slowly closed the gap between her and Donna Silver, and all the kids around me screamed even louder, and I decided I didn't care if Effie didn't speak to me for a whole year, if only she would win, and then I thought, no, better that she should make up with me, even if that meant she would lose the race, because what would I do if Effie didn't talk to me for a whole year, and I didn't get how you could want a thing and want the opposite of that thing at the exact same time.

And then she won. Adam once said that thoughts could go from one head to another and change things, and I hoped that my good thoughts had defeated the mean ones and reached Effie and helped her to win. But when everyone hugged her I stayed on the side. A whole year without Effie! Oh boy.

CHAPTER 6

"Tell her that I say congratulations," I said to Brody the next day at recess.

Brody went to Effie and told her that Julie said congratulations. So she wouldn't have to look at me, Effie climbed to the top of the monkey bars in the first-grade playground. "Yeah," she said, but you could see that Effie didn't have much experience staying mad.

I asked, "What's her problem, anyway? She loved the chocolate and the balloons. And besides, she won the race."

Brody went and told her what I said, and Effie was quiet for a bit, and then she told him, "She wanted me to lose the race."

"Effie!" I wailed, and I took a step toward her, but she quickly moved to the other side of the ladder and said to Brody, "Even that time when I raced against her ugly dog, she wanted me to lose."

Brody came back to me and said, "You should have told Blue Dawn that it was you."

"But it wasn't me," I said. Effie held on to the bar with only one arm and swayed back and forth in the air.

"Because of you she made Effie miss recess and she almost made her miss the race," Brody said.

"No. Not because of me."

"Then because of who?" Brody asked.

"I don't know," I said. "And now go back and ask her about the notes she got, with the scribbles on them. What was written in the last note, the one she made into a paper airplane?"

"Ask yourself," Brody said. "You wrote them."

I ran past Brody until I reached the ladder that Effie was climbing.

"Come down, Effie," I said.

Effie didn't answer, and I saw that she wanted to keep on climbing but there was nowhere left to go. Above her there was only a tree, and when I looked up at her from below, her face looked black because of the branches and the shadows, and she said, "You're just like Donna Silver. You think I'm a baby. And stupid."

"There's nothing wrong with being a baby. It's not so bad at all," I told her. "Come on, Effie. Come down. You're not stupid."

But Effie said I should get out of her sight, so I walked away thinking that it might really take a whole year before Effie forgave me, but still I went and asked all the kids if they knew anything about the presents Effie got, and mostly about those scribbled notes, in handwriting you could barely read.

The only one who was willing to discuss this with me was Adam. He didn't know much about the scribbles, but he sure knew all about scrambled eggs, including the scientifically proven fact that if you ate too many scrambled eggs at one meal, you lost your hold on gravity and you might even begin to float away a little, but only if you were really high up. And that was why you often saw mountain climbers going up the Himalayas with cartons of eggs, because they wanted to get right to the summit and then rise up a little more. "And do you g-get what a g-g-g-great feeling that is? To f-f-float in the air in the highest place on earth?"

"Enough already, Adam!" I said. My cousin, who hadn't eaten any eggs, was floating at this very moment on the monkey bars and wouldn't even look at me. I stood there totally disheartened, watching the boys play soccer. Scribbles, I thought. Handwriting so bad that you could hardly read it . . . Something was humming in my head, and I was beginning to get an idea about what it was telling me, and I started moving really quickly between the shoulders and the legs that were in motion all over the soccer field, and I grabbed Danny by the sleeve—one second before he kicked the ball—and I said to him, "It's you."

The other boys yelled at me to get off the field, but I had no intention of moving. I tugged on Danny's shirt and dragged him aside. He stared at me in shock, and I said to him, "How much wood . . . ," and by the look on his face I saw that I was right, that it really was him.

Danny told me that Blue Dawn the principal talked to him after he made Effie fall that day and told him his punishment was to do some nice things for Effie, simple as that. So he decided to buy her chocolate and balloons but not to let her know that they were from him. And on the notes, he wrote in his terrible handwriting, "How much wood would a woodchuck chuck if a woodchuck could chuck wood?" because he couldn't get it out of his head ever since the kids in first grade told everyone that about 2,500 years ago students used to yell it on field trips.

I told him that he had always been a miserable creature, and that once he may have been miserable, mean, and violent, and now maybe he wasn't as violent as he used to be. "But still, I don't like you," I said. "You're a miserable lost case. And stupid." Danny smiled as if I had said something really nice, and I tried but I really couldn't be mad at him.

Then all the soccer players crowded around us, so Danny gave me a push but it didn't hurt, and I pushed him back, and that was how we made it look like we were fighting, so no one would notice anything, and Danny ran onto the field without turning back, and I walked away slowly and quietly and tried not to jump for joy, and all I wanted to do was find Effie and help her down from the top of that ladder.

In the afternoon, when we were both in the backyard, Effie was in a good mood, and she wanted to talk. We sat under the big tree, and she stroked Shakshuka and gave her the hairdo of a princess, and said, "You have to want *me* to win the races. I'm your cousin."

"But Shakshuka's my dog," I said.

"But I'm your cousin," Effie said. "And besides, Shakshuka is never happy when she wins. She doesn't even know that she's won. So you should root for me."

Brody said that even when Danny tried to do something nice, it always turned into a disaster. I guess that was true. There were kids who always did good deeds, and others who always caused problems, and then the principal put her heavy hand on their shoulder, and they promised to be good. Danny was like that. Sometimes I passed him in the corridor, and when no one was looking, I said, "How much wood . . ." just to annoy him, and he said that was not the way to say it, that I had no sense of rhythm, but he was obviously wrong because how could anyone mess up a tongue twister if they got the words right?

When we ran races behind our building, Shakshuka usually beat Effie, and sometimes I rooted for Effie but not always.

I also didn't care when my musical cube broke one day after I gave it to the Munchkins. It might have been a smart toy, but Monty was smarter and he managed to take it apart and pull out the noisy piece, and he was happy because every time he shook it, the music played, and Max began to dance and Monty clapped his hands, and Mom just sighed and said, "Why is it always the worst toys that live forever? Am I going to have to listen to that terrible noise for the rest of my life?"

But Mom should have known better. After all, she was the one who always said that you had to choose which things to take to heart.

SHAKSHUKA AND THE REALLY EVIL CAT

CHAPTER 1

Nobody believed it when Effie decided to be best friends with Donna Silver, but that was exactly what happened. And nobody believed Adam when he told us that the security guard at our school was once a brilliant professor but now she was a member of a gang of jewel thieves, and I still didn't believe it, well, okay, maybe a bit. And nobody would have believed that my dog, Shakshuka, would bring home a cat, a nasty cat that didn't like anyone, but she did, and we adopted him. We made a big mistake with that cat, but my mom said that with cats, you couldn't change your mind, and if we got a little devil for a cat, we just had to take care of him and love him the way he was, even if he did have an ice cube where his heart should be, because you didn't choose family, family was something that happened to you, and that was just the way it was.

The cat must have latched on to Shakshuka one day in the yard and followed her home, and when we opened the door she barked as if to tell us to take care of him because he was a kitten, but she also barked at the cat so he wouldn't bug her too much because she wasn't his mother.

But worse than our evil cat was that Effie became friends with Donna Silver. When Donna Silver decided that someone was her friend, that person didn't have room for anybody else. Donna Silver had an invisible circle that surrounded her, and whoever didn't belong couldn't get in, even if that person stood right beside her or sat right beside her in class. And the ones who belonged in her invisible circle were always inside it, even when they were at the other end of the building, and that was how it was from the very first minute, ever since she moved to the neighborhood and started coming to our school. She couldn't run as fast as Effie, this Donna Silver, but she was the girl everyone came to watch when she did the long jump, and the day she broke a record some of the kids from the other class started singing:

"It's Silver, Silver!
Silver, she's the thriller!
And it's Donna, Donna!
Donna who we wanna!"

And that was how it went, on and on, that rhyme, and she brought Effie right over to her side, the side for the best girl athletes, and at recess they walked around holding hands. And Donna always brought huge fruits from home for her snack, peaches the size of soccer balls, and she ate and talked really quietly because that was how she was. Everything she said sounded like a whisper, and Effie listened to her as if there wasn't anybody or anything else in the whole world, and she didn't even blink. When I asked Effie to come over and eat spaghetti with me after school, she could never come because she was walking Donna home.

But that wasn't enough for Donna, and sometimes she got together five or six girls, really close until all their heads were touching, and she was in the middle, whispering something, I never managed to hear what, and the girls were all crowding in to get closer, and then when she was sick of it she pushed them away so shc could have some space.

First she gave one girl a rough shove on her shoulder, saying she couldn't get enough air, and she pushed the girl aside just like you'd push aside a chair that was in your way, but as if it was all a joke. Then the other girls moved away by themselves.

One time I tried to talk to Effie. "What does Donna Silver want with you?" I asked. "You don't make noise, you hardly talk. You're so spacey. And she's a queen. . . ."

Effie said, "I'm also a queen. I'm the fastest runner in the whole school."

"She's a better long jumper," I told her.

"But I'm stronger than she is," Effie said.

"Exactly," I said. "She wants you because you're the best toy there is, the strongest."

"Enough already, Julie," Effie said, and her eyes had that look they got when she was running like the wind, eyes that said, "You can do what you like, but you can't stop me."

"I'm her friend. And you're just mean," she told me.

Brody said I was overreacting, that it would pass. Donna would get tired of Effie and find another girl to be her toy. "And anyway, what do you expect?" he said. "You think she should hang around just because she's your cousin? You don't even notice her most of the time, she's just like Shakshuka for you, but now just because she's hanging around with Donna, you're starting to go nuts." Brody was like that, he always said the worst things, but he was still my friend and besides, there was nothing I could do about Effie.

I told him he didn't know what he was talking about, that you couldn't compare a dog with a cousin. It was true that they both ran fast and didn't talk much, but other than that, they weren't anything alike.

Brody thought I was jealous. But why should I be? Should I be jealous of the strawberries that Donna Silver ate at recess, which were so red you couldn't believe it, each one like a fat, smiling heart? Strawberries were just fruit. No, it was only that I was worried about Effie because Donna Silver could be really nasty, and she once said that Effie's legs might run fast but the rest was too slow, only nobody remembered that except for me.

Even Effie didn't remember. Today she passed me going down the stairs and other than a tiny "hi," we didn't say anything, just looked at each other and quickly looked away. Brody didn't understand anything if he thought Shakshuka and Effie were the same thing. Shakshuka would never walk past me as if she didn't know me.

I went out to the yard and looked down so I wouldn't have to see anyone and I tried to just watch where I was putting my feet, but I couldn't help it and I looked up once, and of course there was Danny coming toward me. It was amazing how Blue Dawn had managed to totally wear him down with all her anti-violence talk. Now she was on to something new and she was always talking about how we had to give each other personal space, which meant you couldn't push or crowd together or hug each other without permission, and for sure you couldn't hit anyone.

So Danny hardly hit anymore, but he had to cause trouble somehow, so he pushed stuff off my desk, and once he put a ladybug in my pencil case, and now when he saw me he shot out his leg in the air as if he was about to kick a soccer ball and managed to step on my foot because with him there was no such thing as personal space. And then he said, "Oops, sorry, that was an accident."

"You're such a pain," I told him.

Danny asked, "What happened to your hands?"

"My cat scratched me," I said, and I turned my hands over to show him all the scratches.

"You have an attack cat," Danny said. "What do you want with a cat like that?"

I explained to him that my mother thought if we got an evil cat, it must have been what we deserved. Danny listened to my explanation and then stepped on my foot again, pretending it was another accident. "Enough, it hurts," I said. "You're the one who deserves a cat like that. Maybe you want him?"

Danny didn't answer. He saw his friends in the distance, and that was the end of the conversation. As he walked away, I shouted after him, "That cat would really suit you! His head is also as empty as a soccer ball."

Just then I saw Adam standing with some kids near the water fountain, telling them that the security guard at the gate to our school was once a genius professor until she realized that she had special powers.

I tried to picture the security guard, who sat by the gate chewing gum and fiddling with a big bunch of keys, and I thought she didn't look anything like a professor, but Adam said it was one hundred percent true, she was once a great professor, and lots of people said she was the smartest woman in the country, but then she discovered that she could see through walls, and at first it drove her completely crazy because she'd go walking down the street and without meaning to, she could see the people inside their houses, and so as not to spy on them she tried closing her eyes, but even through closed eyes she could see everything, and in the end she realized that she could be really rich, and she joined a gang of thieves and they divided up the work—she looked through the walls of the houses to where the diamonds and gold were hidden, while the thieves went in during the night and took them, and afterward they divided up what they stole, and now she really was a rich woman, but she worked as a security guard so no one would suspect her.

"So of all things she chose to work as a guard?" Brody was surprised.

"That's how she r-r-relaxes," Adam explained. "The noise the kids make r-relaxes her."

Brody said he didn't believe a word, and I felt the same, but still I went over to look at her from where she couldn't see me. Adam usually talked about things that happened far away, things that you couldn't see, but this time we could see that security guard with our own eyes.

"Do you think she looks like the smartest woman in the country?" I asked.

"If Adam says so, it must be true," said Brody sarcastically, but still we decided that tomorrow we'd get up early in the morning and have a look around the gate to see what the security guard was doing. We didn't know exactly what we were hoping to find, and Brody said that she certainly wouldn't hide the gold and diamonds in her little wooden booth, but we figured we'd have a look anyway. What did we have to lose?

CHAPTER 2

When I got home, I went all the way around the kitchen so I wouldn't have to walk past the cat and I gave Shakshuka a hug. I had to admit, the cat was really beautiful, and sometimes he looked at everything through half-closed eyes and seemed perfectly happy, as though he'd never seen anything so pretty before in his whole life, as if there was nothing lovelier than the garbage cans in our yard, the waist-high weeds, the fence with the peeling paint, and when he was in that kind of mood you could even stroke him and he purred, but after a little while he started to scratch you for no reason, and maybe because of that we still hadn't found a name for him because to give someone a name you had to spend time with him, and the Munchkins and I always ran away from the cat before that could happen.

Sometimes Monty just couldn't help himself and he touched the cat, and the cat couldn't have cared less that Monty was just a baby and he scratched him too. Max crawled out of the cat's way as fast as he could, to be on the safe side, and when he did that he looked like a small animal running away from a big, strong animal. And sometimes when the cat walked past him, Max turned to stone and looked at the cat without moving his eyes, convinced that the cat was a tiger and that he, Max, was a little boy in the jungle, and somehow he understood, or maybe it was just his baby body that understood, that it was better not to move and then the tiger wouldn't hurt him because it would think he was a tree or a rock.

Mom said that from a young age, kids needed to understand that the world wasn't a perfect place, and that not everything in life was fair, and that was the reason people chose cats for pets. And Dad laughed. Dad was the kind of person who took things in stride. He was the only one who dared to pick up the cat, he didn't mind getting scratched, and he was the one who went and bought him a red collar and wrote "Cat" on it, along with our phone number, so that if the cat ever got lost and people found him, they'd know what kind of animal they found.

Shakshuka also took the cat in stride. At first she would get mad at him every time he jumped on the table or on the kitchen counters, and that was how he learned that he wasn't allowed to do that, but now they played together like best friends, and when you watched them, it was hard to tell whether she was the one who adopted the cat or the cat was the one who adopted her.

That was how it was. Everybody except for me seemed to know how to take things in stride. I sat on the floor under the table so I could be with Shakshuka, and I told her that she was probably the best dog in the world for adopting such an evil cat. I could never be as nice as she was. Maybe my dog could teach me how to become more generous. If you asked me, I'd say that cat should be sent back to where he came from, returned to I didn't care where, but there was nowhere to return him to, and anyway, nobody was asking me.

● ● ●

In the morning, Brody and I got to school early and we saw that a pipe had burst in the middle of the little kids' yard, and the water was flowing like a stream under the high monkey bars. Someone standing next to us said that soon workers would come to fix it, but then Brody jabbed me with his elbow and said, "Look," and I looked and saw the security guard with a wrench in her hand, her legs soaked to her knees, fixing the pipe herself.

"N-n-no surprise," said Adam, who arrived at just that minute, hopped over the new stream, and already knew exactly what was going on. "Our security guard has golden hands. With those hands, she breaks into houses. Maybe she's the one who caused the pipe to burst in the first place, you know. Maybe it's all part of her plan. Maybe she and the other thieves go through the pipes under the ground to get into the building where the bank is, at the end of the block."

"Wait a minute," Brody said. "First you said that she only looks through the walls to see where the gold is, and the other thieves go and steal it. You said she doesn't break into the houses herself. So how does she suddenly have golden hands?"

Adam said it was true, that was the way they divided up the work in the beginning, until she discovered that they were cheating her—she would show them where the gold was and then she'd go home, and they would do the stealing and keep everything for themselves, without leaving her anything. That was when she decided to break in along with them, and because she was such a brilliant professor, she became the best burglar.

●◉●

At morning recess, Donna Silver came right up to us. At first she stood quietly, watching Adam trying to separate his sandwich from its paper wrapping, and then she asked what the story was with this kid, so Brody explained very seriously that this week it was our turn to look after Adam, and that we took turns in our class because he always had to have someone watching over him, otherwise he went around bumping into trees and poles, or filling his pockets with dirt.

Adam made strange faces and looked up at the sky and pretended he was trying to bite my shoulder, and I gave him a little slap as if I was angry, and we all thought we were putting on a really good show, but Donna Silver wasn't impressed at all, she just whispered, "Yeah, yeah, very funny," and strolled along with a forgiving smile on her face.

After that, we saw Blue Dawn the principal coming, so we hid behind the greenhouse that the nature teacher built because we weren't in the mood to hear her explain again about our friends' personal space and how it had to be respected and protected, and I told Brody and Adam that the problem with our new cat was that he liked his personal space too much, and sometimes he lay down in the middle of the hall and didn't let anyone pass by, and if they did, he put on his warrior expression and hissed like mad.

"See how everyone respects the principal's personal space?" asked Brody. "Wherever she goes, everyone disappears."

But not everyone disappeared. Of all the people in the world it was the security guard who stood talking with the principal. It was quiet for a minute and we could hear the principal saying, "They're dangerous, aren't they? They climb up and get into everything. They'd better not get into the classrooms." And after that we couldn't hear anything.

But that was more than enough for Adam, and he said that now it was all crystal clear. "Blue Dawn wants to know everything about the gang of thieves because now she's partners with the security guard."

"Blue Dawn is a diamond thief?" Brody laughed. "No chance."

But Adam explained that Blue Dawn couldn't care less about jewels, that was obvious. It was just that she didn't want dangerous robbers running around the school. All she wanted was for the security guard to look through the walls and tell her what was going on in the classrooms when the doors were closed, who wasn't paying attention and who was making trouble, because Blue Dawn had to know everything, that was how it was, the whole world was her personal space.

During homeroom with our teacher, Mrs. Brown, I made a tiny braid in my hair like the ones Effie always made, and I tried to tie it with a blue elastic, but Danny stole it from me, so I threw an eraser at him, and then he hid the eraser, and I had to scream at him to get it back. There was no such thing as personal space in this world, I thought. Someone just made that up.

At the next recess I saw all the girls standing in a circle with Donna Silver in the middle, and I saw how she was sick of the whole thing and she pushed them, one by one, as if she was joking around, and then pulled Effie along behind her, and they walked away with their arms around each other. And later I saw her standing in the middle of the yard, stretching her arms out to her sides and spinning around faster and faster, just like Shakshuka used to do when she was a puppy, but without the arms. Shakshuka used to chase her tail, but Donna Silver didn't have a tail, she just spun round and round until she got dizzy and then she flew off to the side, and she wasn't afraid of falling because of course someone would catch her, and this time Brody and Adam happened to be standing there and she fell right on top of them. I was standing on the side and I saw how Brody was holding her and how he had this little smile on his face, and how Donna Silver laughed and said, "Wow, I can hardly breathe. Air. Why isn't there any air here?"

I climbed up to the top of the high monkey bars in the yard, as Effie liked to do, and I stood up there and I ate a cookie that I'd hidden in my sweatshirt pocket, and as I looked at the crumbs falling on the sand, I thought, Oh no, what if Blue Dawn the principal tells me that I have to get down now and find every crumb that fell? How will I find crumbs that got mixed up with the dust and dirt, or that the wind has blown away?

* * *

Later Brody passed me in the hallway, and he said, "Where have you been, anyway?" I didn't even feel like turning around, I just sat on the bench outside the teachers' room as if I was punished, like the kids who had to sit there and wait to have a talk with the principal. Then for the whole recess I made circles on the floor with my feet, thinking about what the principal said to the security guard. They were dangerous, they climbed, they got everywhere. A ray of sunlight came in through the window and hit the floor exactly where my feet were, and I discovered if I moved my feet in circles, I could really see the dust rise in the sunbeams, and that was how I spent the entire recess, and I learned that if you sit quietly you hear lots of things. For example, I heard Adam telling some kids how scientists managed to raise a silkworm in a laboratory that if you put it in a school book, it would crawl across the pages and erase all the boring parts, and Donna Silver said, "If you give me a worm like that, I'll bring you whatever you want."

Adam said, "Wh-wh-whatever I w-w-want?"

And Donna Silver said, "Whatever you want."

Adam said, "Bring m-m-me the silkworm, that's wh-what I want."

And Donna Silver couldn't stop laughing. Even when she laughed it sounded like she was whispering. That girl, you could hardly hear her, and still the whole school was full of her.

CHAPTER 3

On the way home, Brody said, "Leave Effie alone already. She doesn't have to stick to you like glue."

I said, "I'm used to her coming over to eat spaghetti. I'm used to her being Effie, and now she's not Effie."

"She doesn't have to be Effie just because you're used to it," Brody said.

"You're also friends with Donna Silver now," I said. "I saw her spinning around and then she fell on top of you."

"What do you want?" said Brody. "It's not my fault that she fell on me."

"Air, air!" I said. "I can hardly breathe. Why isn't there any air here?"

"You don't know how to talk like her," said Brody, whispering, "Air, move aside, I need air!"

He started to collapse in a faint but stopped himself before he hit the sidewalk. I laughed, but it didn't help. Brody had stepped inside Donna Silver's invisible circle, and even Adam managed to get to her with his stories. Let them all be with her. Who needed them?

●●●

At home I tried to be like Dad, who somehow managed to win over the cat by stroking him. I patted him, and at first it was fine, but then something annoyed him and he scratched me and I didn't care. I kept on playing with him and he kept on scratching me and he also bit me, and in the end it hurt too much and I lay on the floor and hugged Shakshuka so no one would see that I had tears in my eyes, and Shakshuka licked my cheek and I hid my face in her fur, and Monty came and saw us and he started to clap his hands, he thought it was funny, the way we were all tangled up together, and maybe he was a little worried about me, and then he started to shout "Peekaboo, Julie," and in the end I had to lift my head and say "Peekaboo, Monty," and then I hid my head again, and Monty laughed his head off, and that was how I finished with my crying before it even started.

Later, when I helped Mom put the Munchkins to sleep, I asked her if there was an insult so bad that it never ended, a disappointment that kept hurting. A sadness that never ever ever ever went away.

Mom said she had to think about it because this was a very serious topic. "Toffee!" said Monty, who was listening to us with a sweet, sleepy expression on his face.

"I said, 'topic,' not 'toffee.' Go to sleep!" said Mom.

And Max said, "I don't want toffee. Yuck."

After that Monty managed to pull down the curtain and tried to cover Max because Max liked blankets, but Max didn't want to snuggle under a curtain because a curtain wasn't a blanket, and it took Mom about an hour to hang it again, and after that she had to read them eight bedtime stories because otherwise Max wouldn't fall asleep, and that was the end of my conversation with Mom.

●　●　●

In the morning Danny brought me a thick glove, an oven mitt really, so that I would be able to stroke the cat without getting scratched. I didn't want to ask where it came from or whether he had sneaked it out of his house. I felt it all over and I examined it from all sides.

"What are you worried about?" Danny asked. "I didn't put a mouse inside. Try it on."

I turned it open-side down and shook it, and it was true that there wasn't a mouse inside. Just a beetle.

"You are so dumb," I said to Danny, "that you should win a prize." But I walked around all day wearing that oven mitt, and I didn't take it off even when Adam announced that it reminded him of his uncle, who couldn't stand Chinese green tea.

"That's really sad to hear, Adam," I remarked.

But when Adam got going on a story there was no stopping him, and he kept talking about how his uncle really hated green tea more than anything in the world, but his aunt thought it was healthy and every morning she made him a cup of piping hot Chinese green tea, and when she wasn't looking, he poured it out the window, and that was how it went every day, until once they looked outside and discovered a strange Chinese vegetable growing there that no one recognized, and there was no need to cook it because it grew precooked because of the boiling hot tea, and when they tried to peel it they found it was hot inside as if it had just that minute come out of the oven, and they put it in the fridge but even three days later it was still boiling hot.

Brody came up while Adam was talking and we walked in circles around the water fountain, and we passed underneath the monkey bars in the little kids' yard and stepped in the squishy mud, and suddenly I felt happy. We didn't see Donna Silver and maybe everything would go back to the way it was before. We kept on walking and we went around the soccer field, but Danny wasn't there, and we found ourselves next to the security guard's wooden booth. She was sitting reading a book and chewing gum and playing with her bunch of keys, and Adam said she kept tabs on us wherever we went and she had no problem at all seeing us right through her book.

"But why does she care what we do?" I asked.

Listening to one of Adam's stories was like staring at the last remaining crumbs in a chip bag. Some things you simply couldn't leave unfinished.

Adam explained that the security guard checked out everyone who came near her booth because that was where she hid her diamonds. And some kids told him that yesterday, after everyone went home, they saw her dragging a big sack out of the booth, and they heard weird sounds.

Brody and I said that it didn't make sense to hide diamonds in a place like that, anybody could steal from there, no problem, but Adam said the security guard was smart, she knew that it was the one place where no one would ever think to look.

"And what about Blue Dawn?" I asked.

"B-B-Blue Dawn knows everything," Adam said. "B-but she'll never give her away. That's what you call the p-p-perfect crime."

"That's what you call perfect nonsense," said Brody, who was trying to annoy Adam, but as he said it, he looked hard at the booth, as if there was a chance he might really see the diamonds there. And I think I may also have checked if I could catch a glimpse of them, even though I was definitely not the kind of person who could see through walls.

During the long recess, I went outside and I saw a big group of kids standing in the middle of the yard, and in the center of the center of the center of the group was Adam, and he was talking to Donna Silver, who stood there with Effie, and Donna and Effie had their arms around each other.

Donna completely forgot that just yesterday we tricked her about Adam, and she forgot that he was one of those weird kids you had to feel sorry for, and now she thought he was the cutest kid in the whole grade, and Adam told her that he wasn't so cute, there were much cuter kids, and of course right away that reminded him of a story.

Pretty much all kids were cute when they were in first grade. But a few years ago, there was this kid at our school who started out in first grade as cute as anyone, but in second and third grade he was still like that. He was so incredibly cute that when kids saw him coming they would chase him and kiss him, and at recess there was no chance he would get to play because everyone jumped on him to hug him and he was so miserable that the only day he looked forward to was Halloween so he could wear a costume and no one would recognize him, and on Halloween he came to school in the ugliest, scariest mask, and he wore it everywhere he went and no one knew it was him and no one hugged him, and he was so glad and happy, and he even started wishing that that mask would somehow melt into his face and then everyone would finally leave him alone, but then they had a competition and his costume won second prize and they told him to go up on the stage, and the principal leaned down to shake his hand and knocked off his mask by mistake, and there was perfect silence and everyone was staring at him, and he realized that it had worked—finally he had become an ugly, scary boy—and he smiled. . . .

"And then what happened?" cried some of the kids because Adam had stopped talking.

"Wh-wh-what do you w-want?" Adam asked, looking all wide-eyed and innocent.

"Tell us already. What happened? Did he become as ugly as his mask?"

Adam said that at first, when he saw the expressions on the faces of the people staring at him, he thought that he must look absolutely horrible because everyone looked so shocked, but then he realized that they were astonished to see how totally adorable he seemed because compared to that mask he looked even cuter. It was a disaster, and now he was thirty-seven and people were still following him wherever he went, kissing his cheeks. No one had ever seen such an unhappy guy.

It was quiet. Everyone was thinking about the thirty-seven-year-old cutie pie who had to run away from people in the street.

And then Donna Silver said, "I don't feel sorry for him. I hope I'm cute when I get old." And she looked around to see if anyone would argue with her.

Brody said, "Forget it, no chance. You'll be an ugly old lady," and he bent over and started hobbling around as if he had a backache.

"Oh, you're right. That's how I'll be," whispered Donna Silver, and everyone laughed. Effie laughed too, even though sometimes she was so spacey she didn't notice funny things, and it was only then that I noticed

how far away from everyone else the bench I was lean-
ing on was, and how far away I was, and from the side,
I almost managed to see, like in a cartoon, that invisible circle, which suddenly looked more like Donna
Silver's invisible castle.

CHAPTER 4

And then a terrible noise started and I couldn't hear what everyone was talking about in the invisible castle anymore. The security guard was working with a drill in her booth behind the closed door. I didn't need Adam to guess what was going on in there—I realized that she was digging a tunnel that would lead her right into the coffee shop across the street, and once there she would drill a hole in the cash register and take all the money and no one would notice.

What do I need friends for? I thought. I'd wait until everyone went home, and I'd hide somewhere until the security guard brought out her sack full of diamonds, and that way I'd catch her by myself. So long as her dangerous friends didn't decide to come visit her. But after the last bell rang, after gym, when I ran to my classroom to get my schoolbag, something happened that made me forget all about the security guard. Effie was sitting alone on the highest school step. When she saw me, she asked if she could come over to have spaghetti because Tuesday was always spaghetti day at my house.

I said, "How come you want to come over all of a sudden? Did Donna Silver run out of spaghetti?" And even as I was saying the words, I felt sorry because Effie looked really sad, and when Effie was sad she didn't cry, but sometimes that was even worse, and I walked away fast so I wouldn't see her like that.

Once, a long time ago, Effie came to sleep over and we were playing and we lost track of time and in the end we stayed up all night. At some point Mom walked into the room and told us to go to sleep right away, and we told her that we would, soon, and after that Dad came and he brought us tea and cookies and we ate and talked and played, and somehow the night passed. There was a moment when I realized that it was almost morning, and that no matter what we did, the night was over, gone, and there was no way we were going to get any sleep, and we were awfully tired. Birds were chirping. We stood by the window and saw that the light was starting to push away the darkness—just like Donna Silver pushed the girls at school in her so-called sweet harmless way.

I leaned my head on Effie's shoulder and I felt as if something big was happening, something frightening yet amazing, and I was sure that by sunrise I would understand things and become a grown-up. But then we both fell asleep on the sofa.

I remembered the sleepover as I walked away. I thought, What a shame I didn't invite Effie to come over to eat spaghetti. We had that chocolate with nuts that was her favorite, and I hid it high up so the Munchkins wouldn't find it. I could have given her chocolate and we could have made up. I dragged one foot behind the other down the corridor, and I pretended that I wasn't allowed to lift my feet off the floor, and I thought about how I could still manage to move from place to place, and I tried to move as if someone was pulling me along, as if each of my knees weighed a ton, and I was glad that no one could see me. The building was almost empty. The cleaners hadn't arrived yet. One kid ran fast to his classroom; he must have forgotten something. From the yard I could hear the sounds of kids going home. The corridor was long and seemed never-ending. I peeked into the classrooms and saw orange peels, empty bottles, a shirt thrown over a chair, and every class looked like a different country.

And I saw Donna Silver. She came toward me down the hallway half running and half dancing, thrusting out her long arms, one in front of her and one behind. I stood stock-still, but Donna Silver kept on dancing and stopped only after she'd moved a few steps beyond me.

"I know who you are," she said almost in a whisper. "You're Effie's cousin. Here!" And she threw me a huge apple, as big as a grapefruit. I barely caught it. It was red and it smelled fantastic, like pink bubble gum, like leaves and earth and rain, as though it had just that minute been picked from the tree.

What would happen if I was friends with Donna Silver? At recess she would put her hand on my shoulder or lean against me, and she would say funny things, and I would feel like I belonged, without doing anything at all.

I didn't have a chance to say thanks. Donna Silver floated away.

• ● •

Outside, by the gate, I remembered Adam's story. I stopped and kneeled to fix one of my socks that had slipped down into my shoe, and I peeked into the booth right under the nose of the security guard, who was sitting and reading the paper and playing with her keys, and I managed to see that there really was a big red sack inside, and I knew that I'd seen that sack someplace before but I couldn't remember where. If only I could see through walls, or at least through sacks, I thought, and I straightened up quickly because I was afraid that the security guard would look at me and see my thoughts, just like she saw diamonds. What should I do now? Hide and wait, I guess. But my head felt as if it was spinning round and my legs took me home.

* * *

"Hey, what's wrong with you?" said Mom the minute I walked through the door. And even before she touched my forehead, she announced that I had a temperature, she could tell by my bright eyes. "Please crawl right into bed, and in a minute I'll bring you some tea with honey." I lay in bed, and Shakshuka came to make me feel better, and when Mom wasn't looking I let her climb up on the blanket and lie down next to my legs, and I slept like that for hours and hours, Mom said for almost two days straight, with a few breaks, and I didn't dream about anything, and I didn't care what horrible things the security guard might be getting up to in the meantime, and once I woke up and played pick-up sticks with Dad until the cat came and scattered all the sticks and won the game, and another time I opened my eyes and sat up in bed and I didn't know if it was day or night or what day it was. Shakshuka sat on the floor and looked at me. "What happened, Shakshuka?"

Shakshuka wagged her tail and squeaked a little, as if she wanted to say something.

"I'm telling you," I said, and I patted her, "that you would also be friends with Donna Silver, I promise you. She would whisper something funny to you and you'd go running after her right away. No one can resist her."

But Shakshuka got angry and she gave a loud bark. She wanted to say no, that she would always stay loyal, because that was the way it was with dogs. And she also told me to get up. I got up and followed her, but on the way the cat came and blocked my path and looked at me with his yellow-green eyes and moved his tail that looked like a nervous snake from side to side.

I wanted to go around him, but the minute I moved, he said, "Meow."

I said, "What, again with your personal space?"

"Meow."

"Meow yourself."

And it was only then that I heard someone ringing the bell, and Mom shouted from the kitchen, "Will you get the door, Julie?" and I took two steps back and then I ran forward and sailed over the cat in one giant leap and rushed to open the door for Danny because Mrs. Brown had sent him to bring me the homework.

"She told *you* to come?" I asked in surprise.

"First she asked Effie, but Effie said she didn't want to, or she couldn't, or something like that," Danny said.

"Yes," I said. "Effie doesn't have time for me."

"I don't know what your problem is with this cat," Danny said, petting him. "He's just fine." And he was right. That evil cat suddenly didn't care about his personal space, and he wound himself around Danny's legs, asking to be stroked, and Danny patted him without any oven mitt, and the cat purred so loudly he sounded almost like the security guard's drill.

"Ha!" I laughed. "I knew the two of you would get along!"

"Yeah, but he's smarter."

"Tell me, what does it feel like when you hit somebody?"

"Why, you feel like fighting?"

"What's better?" I continued. "To hit someone or to throw something at them?"

"I don't know," said Danny. "Pushing is also good sometimes."

"Oh, well, maybe I won't hit anyone," I said, "but sometimes I get so sick and tired of them. They're not my friends anymore, and anyway they're all so boring these days."

Danny didn't say anything. He didn't ask who I was talking about. Even Danny understood things sometimes.

Danny said, "So who will you hang around with?"

"Not with the baboons who play soccer, that's for sure," I told him.

"We wouldn't let you either," Danny said.

"Of course not. I'm not dumb enough."

"But your cat is dumb," said Danny because he had to get back at me.

"Well, yeah, that's true," I said to let him win, and I leaned down and stroked that evil cat, but I pulled my hand back double quick because you never could tell with him.

CHAPTER 5

"Let's say we hold a competition," I said to Mom before bedtime, while Dad was giving Monty and Max their bath. "For the worst creature in the house. The worst behavior-wise, the worst in helping around the house . . . the one who makes the most trouble, basically."

"You're raising a very serious topic here," said Mom. "That's not an easy thing to decide."

"It is an easy thing to decide."

"Let's see, Monty wrecks the house, so he must be the winner of the competition. On the other hand, maybe Max is the winner because he never eats anything and it takes him hours to fall asleep. He makes terrible trouble. And the minute he drops off, Shakshuka starts to bark and she wakes him up. Shakshuka's the worst. No! You're the worst because you have the most holes in your socks," said Mom, and she grabbed my feet and tickled me through the holes in my socks. That was my mom. She made a joke out of everything.

The worst creature in the house walked by in the hall, with his tail standing straight up, looking like the scary tip of a shark's fin that you could see sticking out of the water.

"You're better," said Mom. "School tomorrow."

● ● ●

In the morning I decided: Today I'm not going to talk to anyone. Nothing, not a word.

In gym they sang:

> *"Silver, Silver*
> *Flowing like a river."*

And again:

> *"Silver, Silver*
> *Silver is the thriller.*
> *Yeah, it's Donna, Donna,*
> *Donna who we wanna."*

And it went on and on, and it just so happened that I was standing next to Effie when Donna Silver broke her own record for the long jump.

"Your friend's really good," I said.

I was surprised to hear myself talking after all.

"She's not my friend anymore," said Effie, and she jumped in the air and clapped her hands like all the other kids were doing.

I didn't say anything. I remembered how on the last day before I got sick I met Effie sitting on the highest step, all alone, and how she wanted to come over to eat spaghetti and I said no.

I said, "She's the one who's losing out, that Donna Silver."

Effie said, "She never loses."

"She lost you," I said.

Donna Silver was hugging a red-haired girl from the other class. Everything about her is being on top, I thought. No wonder she's such a good long jumper. "So what?" said Effie as if she could hear my thoughts. "I'm losing out too."

When we walked home from school that day, we forgot all about the security guard because Adam was in the middle of a story about some factory near his house that recycled chewing gum, and whoever brought old gum there got a new piece of gum in its place, and once Adam peeked into the back side of the factory and saw a huge pot that took up half the room and a small flame was burning underneath it, and there was a man standing there stirring all the gum together to recycle it and make new gum out of it, and from the bits of the bits that were left over, according to Adam, they made car tires. So the next time we had a piece of gum, we should know that someone else had already chewed it.

Brody said that recycling was definitely very important, but still maybe Adam should stop recycling his stories, and I said that the story actually made me feel like chewing some gum, and only Effie, who was walking along daydreaming and not listening to us, stopped suddenly and said, "Look."

We turned around and we saw. The yard was empty. Everyone had gone home. Almost.

"Be quiet," I said, and I started to walk back, and I didn't even stop to make sure that they were following me. In a minute we were standing outside the locked gate and we saw that there were cats all over the place. Here they are, I thought—the dangerous robbers the principal was talking about, the climbers, the ones who might sneak into classrooms—and I counted seven, each one in a different spot. The security guard had made little piles of food for them all over the yard so they wouldn't fight. There were black-and-white ones, striped ones, one that was completely white, and a beautiful orange one that looked exactly like Donna Silver's new friend. On the side I saw a red sack full of food that looked just like the one we had at home, which Mom bought for the cat. I knew I'd seen that bag somewhere before.

"Good for you, Adam. The security guard's our 'criminal,' " said Brody. "And here are the wicked robbers, eating their lunch." Adam didn't say anything, but his face looked so full of happiness, it was as if someone had switched on a light inside him. If I'd known how to look into kids' heads to see their thoughts, like the security guard could see through walls, maybe I could have seen how he was making up his next story.

"What do you want from Adam?" I said to Brody. "He was right. She may not be a diamond thief, but she's still the smartest woman in the world." And we all watched as the security guard stroked the beautiful ginger cat.

Brody said, "I thought you didn't like cats, ever since you found your awful one."

"What, you have a cat?" Effie woke up.

"I have a tiger," I said, and I gave Effie's shoulder a

head-butt, but not a real one, just a joking one. "Anyone want to come over for spaghetti?" And I saw that Effie would come, and I didn't care about anything else.

We went to my house, Effie, Brody, Adam, and me, and I showed them all how I used the oven mitt that Danny brought me to pat our creature who we still hadn't found a name for, who really was evil and had an ice-cold heart, there was nothing you could do about it, but sometimes he looked at the world with this dreamy, enchanted expression, as if he had never seen such beauty before in all his life, and once I sat down next to him and explained to him that he should learn from Shakshuka, who couldn't care less about personal space, and you could get as close to her as you liked, and Mom saw me talking to the cat and asked if I'd finally made up with him, and I told her that was a serious matter for debate and I really had to think about it.

ACKNOWLEDGMENTS

I was born in a small communal village called a kibbutz, in Israel. As a child I spent many hours every day playing with the other kids in a lush, almost vehicle-free environment, where doors were never locked and secrets were hard to keep. Pets were unleashed, and they often wandered about freely. It was not a perfect childhood, and my own kids were raised in a far more conventional way, much like the characters in my books. Yet some of the kibbutz's free spirit can be found in the world of Julie, Adam, Effie, and Brody in *Dog Trouble!*

I wish to thank my Israeli editors, Rachela Zandbank and Einat Niv, and all the good people at Keter Books for their dedication and friendship. I cherish the advice and support of my wonderful agent, Deborah Harris. I will always be thankful to Erica Rand Silverman, who was the first to read the English manuscript and thought it was funny. I'm grateful to Phoebe Yeh, the editor of this book, for being the profound reader and generous person she is. And I thank everyone else at Crown/Random House for their tireless efforts.

To my sweetheart husband, Amit; my beloved, gorgeous, witty son and daughter, Alon and Yael; my humble dog, Mishmish; and my awful but charming cat—you've all taught me what happiness is. Even the cat . . . Thank you.

ABOUT THE AUTHOR

Galia Oz is a prizewinning children's writer and a documentary filmmaker. She is the recipient of the Levi Eshkol Prize for Literary Works, and her Shakshuka books are some of the most beloved stories in Israel children's literature. Julie's dog troubles have also been published in France, Spain, and Brazil. Oz lives near Tel Aviv with her family, (not so) evil cat, and only sometimes troublesome dog.